ALEXIS PLIGHT

SCI-FI EROTIC ROMANCE

CANDRA AUBREY

plicit Press

CHAPTER 1

THE SUN RISES SLOWLY over the buildings of New York City, creeping into windows and under the cracks in the doors. It's another early morning for Alexis, one of five that she absolutely loves. She's been up since 4:20 AM, ten minutes before her alarm goes off.

It's 2099, and little has changed since 2000. The last hundred years have not seen the advent of teleportation or flying cars. There have been technological advances, but nothing too dramatic, and certainly nothing as eventful as a levitating motor vehicle.

Alexis (she hates being called Alex, which is what everyone who thinks they know her calls her anyway) is on her first cup of coffee when the alarm buzzes to life. She goes and finds it in the bedroom, turns it off, and returns to her ritual of waking up. Not that she's had much trouble waking up, not since, at the tender age of twenty-six, she was appointed senior archeologist with the World Government.

After her second cup of coffee, Alexis does yoga, not because she needs to, but because she needs to pass the time until it is acceptable to walk through the doors at the World Government. It relaxes her enough to make the wait bearable. By 6:30 Alexis is exiting her building in Manhattan's Upper East Side and hailing a taxi.

The World Government's headquarters is in downtown New York. Now, this part of the city has changed. Many of the buildings have been brought down and replaced with newer, shinier ones. Where new structures were not erected in the place of the old there are sprawling gardens. Everybody said it wouldn't be possible. But The World Government decided otherwise.

Paving is everywhere, the streets around the building are no more; just gardens and paving. And beams! Hundreds of invisible beams explain why you don't see anyone in the World Government's gardens, except for maintenance when this is required. And even the maintenance is kept to a minimum thanks to the chosen flora and fauna.

There are several checkpoints, seven in total before you even get into the building. Alexis's cab is stopped at the first one. She always chooses to go the rest of the way on foot just because it's quicker, unless of course it's raining, which it seems to be doing more and more often these days in New York.

The building is accessed thanks to an elaborate biometric system. And once inside, you are not allowed to access any of the parts of the building that have nothing to do with your job. So Alexis passes three more security stations thanks to her index finger and a retinal scan, and then makes her way to the basement.

It's called the basement for no reason other than that it

is technically under the building. Four floors in total make up the World Government's archeological division. No windows to the outside world, no air except for what they themselves supply. This is to preserve the many artifacts housed there, from all over the world. This is Alexis's playground, save for the two lowest stories that her finger and eye print will still not get her into.

She is having her fifth cup of coffee for the morning, her first at the World Government Headquarters, by 8:05! If, like today, she isn't expecting a shipment from some remote part of the world, or from some or other museum, the day will usually involve cataloging the stuff she has, and using it to make sense of life on earth since time immemorial. Already she is thinking of ways that the pieces of the human puzzle fit together. It has become her life's work. But she keeps coming up short, with glaring gaps in the puzzle, gaps she knows she can fill.

She is very systematic and thorough. Alexis goes through a Mayan shipment she received a week before and is interested in the calendar. It makes sense, to a point, even pointing out two catastrophic events that practically brought the planet to a standstill. And since the calendar predates both events, and since she knows that both events actually did happen-one asteroid-one flood-she is certain that the Mayans had a way of predicting the future. This is uncanny, especially in a world that has reduced the bible to a very colorful fairytale.

.   .   .

"Hello, Alex. Coffee?" Her assistant is an enthusiastic third-year archeology student named Zach. He wants to be out in the field, doing real archeology work. But he drew the short straw and now he has to come to the World Government's Headquarters for half a day, three out of the five days that Alexis is working. Alexis cringes at the all too familiar 'Alex' and simply raises her cup for him to take and fill.

Alexis turns the calendar over and over between her fingers. It's a beautiful bronze plaque that fits nicely in her hands. She wonders how long it will be before they experience the next tragedy, another prediction on the calendar. But the date for this one has been scraped off, probably from millennia of handling. She returns it to its glass holder and continues with her cataloging.

"So, you ever miss the field?" Zach hands her coffee and throws on a white coat unnecessarily. He really has become very familiar with her in the three weeks that he's been with her. She hates it. She never wanted an assistant to begin with, but the Government insisted that she has one, probably to gain public vote in light of the upcoming elections. America has always been the seat of the World Government, and they intend to keep it that way.

"Not really. This is where the real work is done, where the real magic happens!" Her response borders on sarcastic.

Zach picks up a weapon, a rod that ends in a sharp spear. He presses a button on it and the spear splits suddenly into eight razor-sharp points, nearly taking his hand off. "Careful with that. Go take care of the day's admin, in the office. I have work to do." Alexis has found that the best use for an assistant is in the daily administration, leaving her to play with her toys. Zach mumbles something about this not being what he signed up for and leaves. She picks up the weapon and examines it.

Alexis had no idea that it opens up the way it does. She presses the button again, not noticing it before because it was concealed in the intricate mold work, a scene from a battle long gone, at its base. The weapon retracts into the single spearhead once more. Again she presses the button that Zach stumbled on by accident, and again the eight sharp heads appear. She wonders at this marvel, so futuristic from such a primitive time.

Cataloging has given her a chance to glance at human history for at least 20 000 years. She is amazed each time she receives a new shipment, from as far a field as Asia, at how the ancient and modern worlds overlapped at points. Alexis finds this strange and fascinating like she is in two eras at the same time.

By the time she is finished with the day's work, it's well past dinner time. She hasn't eaten all day, and save for the constant flow of coffee, she hasn't drank anything either, so absorbed is she in what she does. She stops for a takeaway a couple of blocks from where she lives and eats as she walks, a turkey sandwich on rye. By the time she gets home she has just enough energy for a quick shower and then she falls into her bed, exhausted from the day's excitement.

It's Thursday. Alexis finds herself drawn back over and over again to the calendar. She holds it up to the light, wondering at the part that seems to have been deliberately scratched out. In fact, the more she looks at it, it seems to have been shaved off with a file. But when? And why?

She looks at her private notes. Hundreds and hundreds of pages, squiggles, and notes that she has made since she started working here, trying to find something, anything that will allude to the missing information on the plaque.

"Coffee?" Zach really is over-enthusiastic. She holds up her cup, not to have it replaced, but to show him that it's still more than half full. It's actually cold but she doesn't realize it, not noticing that she has spent a good few hours going through her notes. "I'm gonna get going now if that's okay!" He says this while removing his unnecessary white coat and hanging it up. Alexis just nods him away, not even realizing that he should not have been there today. Monday, Wednesday, and Friday. That was the deal. But he didn't have anything to do today and thought he would come and catch up with the administration. Again something that was totally unnecessary, but he obviously has no life.

"Alexis?" The voice is familiar. She's heard it once or twice before, but never in the lab. So it takes her a minute to place it. It belongs to Grant Chambers, the head of the World Government. She stands up, and almost salutes the man with the graying hair and young face.

"Sir, Mr. Chambers, uhm Mr. President, sir," she stumbles for an appropriate title by which to address him.

"Mr. Chambers is fine my dear. I just thought I'd come down and see what exactly it is you get up to here all alone in the basement." His tone is almost accusing and Alexis feels like she has done something wrong and is about to be reprimanded. Like a child caught with her hand in the cookie jar.

"Mr. Chambers, come in sir." She invites him in although he is already standing beside her in the lab.

"Anything interesting yet my dear?" he asks, again sounding horribly accusing until she realizes that it's the way he ends every sentence with 'my dear' that really bothers her.

"Nothing really sir, mostly I'm just cataloging new shipments. I will begin to make sense of it all in the next few weeks or so." She uses her most composed tone, trying not to give away that she has found glaring gaps in the patterns that she has already discovered. She herself doesn't know yet what it all means so she isn't exactly lying to him, just omitting the truth for now, until she is sure.

He speaks to her of her time spent with them so far as if she has been there forever. He himself has only been with the World Government for a few months, after the untimely death of the previous president. So, since the accident, Grant Chambers is the interim president. Alexis can't help but notice how unfit he seems for the position. He has no bodyguards, almost like he feels that he is invincible, almost as though nothing can get at him. He wears jeans, and a t-shirt that says 'Remember Woodstock', making him look more like the president's rebellious son than the president himself. She shakes this uneasy feeling loose and just responds as best she can to the questions she is asked.

It's not the first time that Grant Chambers has been in

the lab. He was head of the archeological division a while back, but Alexis had never met him. Two people headed up the division after him, something about him needing to take a break, according to the news reports. But if he was so frazzled by simple cataloging, how then was it that he was now the President of the world essentially. Alexis shakes this too, letting it fall to the floor like dust from her coat. Who understands politics anymore anyway? All she knows is that she has her dream job and that is all that matters for the moment.

It is also not the last she sees Grant in the lab. He makes a point of coming down to check on her at least twice a week. This is a mild irritation for her, the feeling that the head of the World Government is looking over her shoulders. She also finds it strange, since she told him that all she was doing was cataloging stuff, and cataloging is so mundane. She would have thought that he had a crush on her if it wasn't that he was apparently happily married to a man.

He finds her alone in the lab on this particular Tuesday. The conversation starts innocently enough until it gets to the point that it always seems to end up at, regardless of how Grant tries to disguise it.

"So, anything interesting yet, my dear?' He asks this question each time he comes into the lab, although offering up various versions of it. But the bottom line is he wants to know if she is making any progress in piecing together the puzzle of human history.

. . .

"No, nothing" is her standard reply to him, although she has the feeling, perhaps because he keeps on asking the question, that she is close to discovering something big, or at least she should be.

"Okay, my dear. Keep up the good work!" He moves out of the room, leaving no traces of himself in it when he does, not even a whiff of cologne. He is a strange man indeed. But one thing becomes clear to Alexis, and that is that she needs to keep her findings to herself for the time being. This could be the find that makes her career. She feels it in her gut.

Tuesdays are nothing special in the lab. But at least it is one of the days that Alexis is alone so that she can focus on finding the connections she so desperately seeks. She needs to know what it is that Grant doesn't want her to find. Or perhaps he wants her to find it. But then why would he keep saying she should keep up the good work when she isn't really delivering anything concrete to them. Perhaps being alone, at work and at home, is just making her paranoid.

At home, she checks her messages. Nothing interesting. Just a guy from one or other insurance companies wanting to confirm when would be the best time to call her. She hates how information is so freely available to these faceless people who call you trying to sell you things that you don't need. She deletes the message and starts cooking while running herself a bath. She really likes to cook, but doesn't do it often enough.

She looks at the counter, next to the kitchen knife. It has a drawing that she made of the weapon that almost left

Zach without fingers. It's not a very good drawing, but it's the best that she could do. She is the first to admit that she is no artist.

Holding it up to the light, as though it was going to suddenly reveal itself to her, she tries to understand how it works exactly. And how a people who were known to cut out the hearts of human sacrifices, and throw people as sacrifices into their only water source, ended up with such a modern piece of weaponry. She takes her wine to the bath while her pasta simmers on the stove.

The World Government sits for their first meeting, one of four that they have every year to make sure that the planet is running smoothly. Representatives from every country are here, but the big guns are still China, Russia, and after a revolution that rocked the continent, Africa. It's a meeting that will last for a week, and the week is one that will be very long.

"The President of our esteemed association, the World Government, The Honorable Grant Chambers," a voice rings out over the elaborate PA system. Grant walks in with a slight swagger, an almost hop in his step that belies the seriousness of this gathering. Translators are in their booths for the benefit of protocol, but everyone speaks English.

"Sit please, my friends. Sit!" Grant is his usual casual self, his t-shirt today reading 'Ruler of the World' unashamedly.

They get into the nitty gritties of economic policy first. This is the quickest part of the week's proceedings since the whole world is now using one currency. Needless to say, it is the dollar. After Grant gets through his updates, he opens the floor for questions, not expecting any.

"What news from archeology," asks China, too soon.

"Nothing. We've placed a young woman as the head of the division who seems to be content with just cataloging. She wouldn't know a discovery if it hit her upside the head. No need to worry." Grant's response is too casual for most of the men and women in the room.

"And we're still just feeding them enough for them to report what we want?" Africa may as well ask since the question seems to be bothering China.

"Just enough to keep them busy. And when they become a little too excited, we'll have her replaced." Grant really sees himself as the ruler of the world. And for all intents and purposes, he is.

A silence comes over the room as though 'replaced' is supposed to hang around and mean something else. It does, and for the rest of the week everyone is careful not to say anything that could get them 'replaced.'

Shipments always hold a special excitement for her. She may not have been at the dig, discovering new things, but she gets to examine them and place them on our timeline. She isn't expecting anything on this particular Monday, but there it is, on her desk when she walks into the office.

. . .

"And this," she asks Zach.

"I don't know; a package I guess. For you," Zach responds while lifting the box and shaking it. Rule number one: Never shake the box!

"Give me that," Alexis says, irritated. She looks at the side of it, the label reading World Government Headquarters. It must be a mistake. She isn't expecting anything today. Fridays have always been shipment days. She wonders if she should open it. Every other box she has received has been clearly labeled 'archeology'. So what if this is a mistake? She turns it carefully over in her hands and then listens to hear nothing inside.

Finally, her curiosity gets the better of her, and after sending Zach to go and get them coffee, she opens it.

Four pieces are in the box, neatly wrapped in bubble wrap. She takes them out, one at a time. Unwrapped, she sees that three of them are tools, or weapons, she isn't sure yet. But it's the fourth piece that grabs her, holding her attention as though a spell has been cast on her. She lifts it up, a heavy bronze plaque with intricate markings. She's seen them before, but for the moment it escapes her.

Then it hits her. She quickly wraps the pieces back up and returns them to the box. She heads to the lab and goes straight for the calendar. She carefully lifts it from its case and places it on a cloth on the table. She unwraps the second plaque and places it above the first on the cloth. Alexis steps back and catches her breath. They are nearly identical.

Alexis examines the new arrival alongside its old counterpart. The newer one is exactly the same as its predecessor except for one thing; it continues. The last date on it is 3000, and what Alexis can make out is that something will end at that time. Perhaps the world, but she isn't sure.

For the next two weeks, she focuses all her energy on this plaque. If she received it by mistake then nobody is saying anything and so she works on it boldly. Even when Grant comes in to find her with it she just carries on working. After all, what can he do? I mean, with all the security measures taken at the World Government, such a mistake shouldn't be possible. And besides, the box contained archeological findings, so who else were they meant for?

3000! The number hangs on her, around her like flies over a carcass. She can't be sure what this means until she has fully deciphered the plaque, but it is possible that it means that the world will end again in less than a year. If so, she really has no time to waste. She needs to un-code it, and then pass the information on to her bosses. Perhaps if they are prepared, then the repercussions of a cataclysmic world's end won't be so bad. She brushes Grant off, saying that she will tell him if she discovers anything, and then gets back to work, leaving him standing and staring at her for a while before he finally gives up and leaves.

. . .

But he has seen what he came to see. And that is a mistake that should not have happened. How did that box end up on Alexis's desk, and not on his? This would be a disaster if she knew what she was actually looking at, but she doesn't. And so everything is fine, at least for a while.

Grant goes straight to the mailroom and demands answers. Nobody knows anything about the box, insisting that Alexis's deliveries are done on Fridays only.

"Then why was the box delivered down to her?" he presses. Still, nobody knows anything about any box. They check their log and there it is, right in front of them, no box came through the mailroom. But then how did that particular box end up in the hands of archeology?

He goes to his office in the penthouse suite. He loves it up here, where he can survey the lay of the land. It feels like he can look over every corner of the world from his perch. No need to get everybody riled up though, at least not yet. He must first find out who put the box on Alexis's desk and take care of them. Then he will turn his attention back to distracting her just enough so that she doesn't stumble accidentally on some unfortunate truth.

Alexis continues her work, despite the distractions of constantly being checked up on by the president himself.

She knows that he will soon become bored with her standard responses and move on to bug someone else. Zach also becomes a mild irritation in the back of her mind, like a fly that buzzes around your head but that you cannot see.

She carefully pieces together the various artifacts that land on her desk, from all over the world. There is definitely a clear pattern forming. But with the glaring gaps, she can't quite make the pieces fit together. But that there has been a system for predicting the future, especially catastrophic events, is abundantly clear.

Jotting down her questions, and making notes, she drinks less coffee. The cups stand on her desk and get cold, and when she requests a fresh cup, Zach's new duty, she leaves this one too to stand and get cold while she peruses her notes. She starts to obsess over the pattern, spending more time at the office than is healthy for anyone.

She wishes she could just dismiss Zach now, needing to concentrate fully on cracking the code of human history. But he is quite capable at the administration, something that she finds herself with less and less time for. So she tolerates him, and he keeps bringing her coffee, which stands, gets cold, and is replaced with a piping hot cup that will just stand and get cold.

On this particular Friday, she leaves the office at 9:45 PM. It's raining out so her taxi has to meet her at the elaborate front entrance to the World Government. She called it an hour earlier, and with the three security checkpoints it takes to get to where she is already waiting on the steps, 9:45 is actually a pretty good time.

She asks him to drive around for a bit so that she takes in the sites of New York, her mind racing. She thinks of the artifacts she left behind at Headquarters. She wishes that she could have snuck out a few that she can work on at home over the weekend, but this is strictly forbidden.

She passes the spot where the Twin Towers once stood, reduced to three gold plaques with the names of all who lost their lives on 9/11. She passes the place where the Statue of Liberty once stood. It's been replaced with a beacon similar to the Washington monument, a structure that seems to serve no real purpose. Time Square is gone too, replaced by parking lots. New York is strange and wonderful and different.

Back in her apartment she goes through her ritual of cooking, bathing, and having a glass of wine, essentially all at the same time. But she is terribly distracted by the information in her head. Could it be that nobody else has ever discovered it before? Could it be that they have, but that it all just ended up nowhere? Could it be a very elaborate cover-up for something more sinister?

Lying in the bath she drifts from dream to dream. Not that she is sleeping. But she is not altogether awake either. Her mind is racing with the possibilities that the information she is gathering quite quickly could have.

After her bath, she settles down to a dinner of wrapped chicken. She pours herself a second glass of wine, feeling reckless, but also just needing to still her mind. The wine has the adverse effect though, and even when she is reading in bed she can't help but think of everything that has crossed her desk, especially in the last few weeks.

She gets up and goes to her desk, a large monstrosity in her bedroom, and looks over the drawings she's made. She has not been able to draw the plaque, but the number 3000 resonates. She holds up a paper with various versions of the number written on it as if it is going to suddenly reveal itself to her.

Saturday mornings are a nightmare. She is up at 4:20 as usual, knowing that she has nowhere to be but wishing that she had. Since it's the weekend her finger won't get her into the building, let alone passed the guards at the first security checkpoints. She makes a mental note to ask for weekend access to the lab and the basement on Monday morning and then tries in vain, as usual, to fall asleep again. With no alarm, no intruding sounds save for the traffic that has become a distant background noise she can't imagine herself living without, she just lies there staring at the ceiling, wanting to be at work, but knowing that she can't be.

Eventually, she just gets out of bed. She tries to do yoga but her concentration isn't there since she is not just buying time until she can walk through the doors at the World Government's headquarters. Unless she managed to do yoga the whole weekend, but even with her daily practice, that would be physically impossible. She makes a fresh pot of coffee and returns to her desk at 5 AM.

By noon she thinks she might just need to eat something and so she pops into the shower. Dressed comfortably she takes to the streets of Manhattan, nowhere in particular in mind, just needing to escape the phantoms she might just have created for herself. She walks past several eateries, eventually settling for a café that has outdoor dining. It's that sort of day.

She finds a spot at a table for two and wonders if she might meet someone interesting today. It isn't something she thinks about often, but while she waits for her food, it's a better thought than work, for the moment.

She looks around at the people in the café and on the street. Men of all shapes and sizes, many variations of a man just going about their Saturday morning, walking around and sitting. She wonders for a moment if they've even noticed her, the girl sitting alone at a table for two, comfortably dressed but not really 'Manhattan'. For a brief moment, she imagines taking one of them home with her, fucking his brains out before the introductions, and then showing him the door before making his acquaintance makes the encounter awkward. But then she dismisses that thought. Too familiar; she's done it a thousand times in her head.

The eggs benedict are good, and so is the carrot and apple smoothie. Good enough for her to forget everything for the moment it takes for her to eat them. Then she orders a coffee and relaxes into the seat, her tablet parked on the table as she checks emails. The waiter's cute she thinks, but far too young to deal with the complexities of a one-night stand.

· · ·

There's nothing of interest in her inbox, and she wonders how it is that she seems to have fallen off the face of the earth, how her friends have all disappeared, or how they are now ignoring her. She needs to make new friends, another mental note.

She logs onto an online dating site where she had planted a profile a while ago but never got around to it. She tinkers around with her profile but makes no attempt to connect with anyone; not even any of the 40 guys who've left her 'winks'. Why can't people just say 'hi' and get the conversation going? What is the purpose of a generic wink? She logs out and returns to her email. Still nothing interesting, no invites to a cocktail or a reunion, no contact made from a long-lost lover. She suddenly feels very old and very forgotten.

She makes a note to contact a few people from her past, who used to be friends. Surely her new job can't have had that adverse effect on her relationships. She also makes a mental note to be nicer to Zach. He's just a wet-nosed kid with an eager mind. And the least she can do is make her contribution to expanding this mind so that he doesn't go out into the real world as wet, or with her as a bitter taste in his mouth!

CHAPTER 2

THE RESEARCH DEPARTMENT of the World Government's archeological division is made up of several researchers from all over the globe. There is just one American on the team, Chloe Harris. Chloe is twenty-four, and highly ambitious. She is also very hot, which seems to be the criteria for working at the World Government if you are a woman.

She pulls her hair into a high, untidy bun, and throws her lab coat on a chair in the lab. The elevator seems to take forever to get her to the ground floor from the basement so she puts her headphones on. As she moves quickly through the various checkpoints that will get her out of the building she doesn't even greet anybody, waving once to the last security guard just because she sees him waving at her. Seven checkpoints on the outside of the building and Chloe is clear of the headquarters. She takes a last look at her emails as the cab she is in turns left and drives in the general direction of the restaurant where she is already late meeting her brother.

. . .

When she arrives for their weekly dinner, a tradition of sorts since their parents died, and since they have no other siblings in the city, her bun is no more. She lets her hair hang loosely on her shoulders as she lets the doorman take her coat. She makes her way through the restaurant and finds Tucker, her older murder detective brother, seated at their usual table.

Tucker is tall with a brooding look, the kind that comes from solving cases for ten years. He was young on the force, joining immediately after high school. At 32 he is young, too young to have already made detective. And Tucker has been a detective since he was 22. He is as ambitious as his sister, but that is the end of their similarities. They are as different as night and day.

"You're late Chloe, and I've got a stakeout later." Tucker sounds more annoyed than he looks, getting up, kissing his sister, and then pulling out a chair for her. He sits only once she is comfortably seated.

"I'm always late. Chill!" Chloe is casual, almost carefree if it wasn't for her mannerisms.

After her first drink, she excuses herself, goes to the bathroom, and emerges her usual, well-put-together self. She sits taller and has regained her composure; leaving the day she's just had in the bathroom.

They go through dinner with the same conversation they always have. It's been four years since the accident that killed their folks and still they refuse to talk about it. They discuss work to the extent that this is allowed and the fact that neither of them has a personal life of which to speak. They discuss the upcoming Christmas holidays that they will both be doing nothing about, yet both claim to have plans. It's just so that they can avoid being together, especially on Christmas day. Neither of them has fully gotten over losing their parents yet and both of them say nothing about it.

When they leave the restaurant Tucker tells his sister to loosen up, and she tells him to get it together. It's the same every time, although it's more likely that Tucker will 'get it together-whatever that means-before his sister loosens up. He walks her to a waiting cab, still full from the fillet of steak and chocolate mousse dessert he's just eaten, and then goes to his stakeout.

Chloe is back in her apartment by ten. She runs a bath while going through the messages on her machine. Two messages are from Tucker reminding her about dinner. She makes a mental note to tell him that he doesn't need to check up on her once a week anymore. Still, she can't bring herself to say 'since her parents died,' even in the safety and comfort of her own home.

She settles into the tub, thinking of a million things. What if she and her brother had decided to go with their parents on the planned second honeymoon as they had been asked? What if she had gone? What if the plane hadn't crashed?

Chloe shifts her attention to something else, quickly.

She wonders how Alexis got her job, at her age, although she can think of one way. But Alexis never came across as that kind of girl. She seems homely, harmless. Maybe it was just her good grades. Maybe it was her application or how she handled the interview. But one thing is certain, Chloe wants her job. Not just because she feels that she would be put to better use as HOD, but because then she will have a workload sufficient to help her forget about her parents.

Fridays are always hectic in the department, with most deliveries arriving on Friday, and so Alexis loves Fridays most of all. Chloe hates Fridays. Simply because there is nothing to do until Tuesday or Wednesday when all has been cataloged. She hates the fact that Alexis, so close to her own age is her boss. But she needs to play nice if her plan to unseat her is going to work.

"Coffee?" Chloe says as she peeks into the door to Alexis's office, holding two coffee cups. They are the paper cups that you get near the machine, the kind you use when you don't have your own coffee mug. Alexis is already drinking coffee from a bright green mug with a cartoon character on the side.

"Yes, sure. Come in!" Alexis is somewhat anxious, taking the cup from Chloe and putting her unfinished coffee down on the table. Chloe greets Zach and then sits down on the sofa in the large office, observing Alexis as she goes through the inventory of expected deliveries for today.

. . .

"Is everything alright," Chloe asks.

"Yes, fine" is the response she gets. Alexis isn't sure yet how she is going to even say what she is thinking and so she doesn't. Chloe and the other researchers are supposed to spend their days in their shared office until Alexis is done cataloging everything because apparently they are all too stupid to tick off boxes. But Alexis is starting to see what the reason behind this rule that she had always thought of as silly is. To have one person accountable for the receipt of these artifacts limits the number of eyes that might see something they shouldn't. And it's easier to get rid of one person. Firing all the researchers would be an HR nightmare.

"So, anything good coming in today, we're getting a little bored in the open plan with the usual savoir fare, and you haven't let us touch anything for a couple of weeks now. Are you sure everything is alright Alex?" Chloe asks.

"Yes, I'm sure. And I thought you still had your hands full with the Chinese artifacts. That was a magnificent find." She tries to sound enthusiastic about the find but it's hard, since it was just hundreds of scrolls, weathered and falling apart, that the research team was supposed to place and piece together.

"I suppose, but do we really all need to be working on those scrolls. I thought I saw a Mayan calendar in the lab. Why can't I take a look at that instead?" Chloe needs something to sink her teeth into while she waits for Alexis to slip up and give her a gap.

"Oh that, it's just a replica of the one we already have." Alexis feels the lie tug at her insides like she's swallowed gum and it got stuck in her windpipe.

Chloe likes her life as it is. Or at least she has accepted it. She has her work and her ambitions. And these fill her days so that she doesn't have to think of her parents at all. But come night time, the nightmares start, almost as if she was there when the plane went down. She tries to drown it out with pills, any pills really, but mostly anti-depressants. 'May Cause Drowsiness' is her favorite line on the prescription bottle. Then at least she goes into a haze that has her thinking it was all just a very bad dream.

At least now she has something else to keep her busy. She knows that Alexis is hiding something. She can feel it deep inside her, in that place that knows. So she decides to 'keep an extra careful eye on her', just in case she lets something slip. But that will have to start on Monday. Right now she has to deal with filling the weekend with distractions.

But Alexis proves to be all the distraction she needs. She sits with her laptop open; pictures of artifacts come into view as a slideshow on the screen. She stares at each one, remembering where each one is from, knowing them all intimately.

She has touched every piece on the screen and analyzed every one. But nothing makes sense to her over and above giving her a look into the lives of humans for the last 20 000 years. Frustrated, she shuts the machine.

"What are you hiding Alex?" she asks herself. And before she can answer her phone rings. It's late, too late for anyone without an intimate association with her to be calling. It's Tucker.

"Hey Chloe, how are you doing?" The voice on the other end sounds like he is talking underwater.

"It's ten o'clock Tucker, and it's Friday. Shouldn't you be out or something?" She is asking herself the question as much as she is asking her brother.

"I know, and I am. I just wanted to check up on you. I was kinda hoping you wouldn't answer, that you'd be off having fun somewhere with your friends?" He lets the question sit for a while, but his sister doesn't take the hint. "Why aren't you out?" he continues.

"I've got something on later. In fact, you're disturbing the process!" By process he assumes her to mean that she's getting ready for the night out, but he knows better. He knows his sister better than she thinks, better than she'd like him to.

. . .

"Chloe you really need to get out more!"

"You mean like you, on a stakeout on a Friday night when you could be, should be, out having fun?" Busted!

"Okay, you got me. But I have to work. And fortunately, we don't all have to keep office hours...Hang on, I've got to go. Call you later." She knows that this means that whatever he was staking out is on the move, so she says goodbye to the dial tone of the telephone. She holds the handset for the longest while and then presses the button that will allow her calls to come through again. Not that she is expecting any calls. Nobody ever calls anymore.

She thinks for a moment of her relationship with her brother, and how they're not as involved in each other's lives as a brother and sister should be. She prefers it this way, but it gets to her sometimes. She just can't let him in, for all his efforts, anticipating the day when she will receive a call that says he's been killed in the line of duty. She can't allow herself to love him with as much attachment as she showed her parents because this way he will be easier to let go of when he dies. She almost expects him to die!

Monday arrives not a moment too soon. By now, Chloe has concluded in her head that Alexis knows something that she's not telling. She's kept the research staff busy with scrolls that could have been the work of two people. And so today, they expect something from her, anything that they can sink their teeth into so that they are not left to their own devices in the open plan.

She walks across the large space and down the short hall that opens up into Alexis's office. Alexis is already at work, trying to come up with something for her research team to do now that they're done with the scrolls. She just needs to keep them busy until she figures out the plaque, and cracks the pattern.

Chloe breathes a smile onto her face, knocks twice on the open door, and then steps inside the office she so desperately wants. "Good morning Alex, how was the weekend?" She asks the question just for the sake of, not really meaning it but asking it anyway.

"Good..." The response is as unconvincing as the question.

Chloe avoids the generic 'so what did you get up to', not wanting to engage with Alexis anymore than she really absolutely has to. She's just here to get their brief for the week, and have a look around the office that will be locked each time Alexis and Zach are out of it. It's not a trust issue. Just that every time you close a door, any door, at the World Government headquarters, it locks automatically, only letting you in if your fingerprint and retinal scan match the ones on file for that specific door.

She scans the surface of Alexis's desk for anything and

comes up short; just Friday's catalog on the surface, with a laptop, a desktop computer, her coffee cup, and a pen. Everything else is neatly filed away thanks to Zach's diligence, and every other thing is put away in the drawers of the desk, thanks to her own.

"So what do you have for us today," Chloe asks, meaning it this time. She is really hoping that they will get to open up the case that houses the two plaques so that they can investigate the new arrival.

"Just a second...come in...take a seat, Chloe." Alexis wishes there was a shortening for Chloe that would make her cringe as much as being called 'Alex' makes her cringe. But she puts it aside and assumes that she is just oversensitive about the issue. But still, she can't help saying 'my name is Alexis' in her head, over and over again, hoping that the present company would read her mind.

Chloe sits at the far end of the sofa in the office and looks around. There are a few staples, a filing cabinet, two desks, chairs, the sofa, a coffee table, and a large painting of a landscape on the wall to make up for the lack of a view. The filing cabinet holds her interest the longest, but she looks away from it each time she feels eyes on her.

But it isn't Alexis's eyes. Zach has been checking her out since she walked into the room. In fact, every Monday since he started working here he's looked forward to Monday mornings the most when Chloe would come in and collect the research team's assignments for the week.

She is stunning. The blonde in her hair is laced with gold, her face beautiful without makeup, a rule that the World

Government has for their female staff as a precaution, for what Alexis is still to find out. She sits on the couch patiently waiting for Alexis to hand over whatever she is busy with, enjoying the attention from Zach, and wondering if maybe, just maybe he might be her way into that filing cabinet. She crosses her legs deliberately, drawing attention to how long they are, firm, tightly wrapped in her skirt, and she watches as the young man's eyes move up over her thighs and linger disappointingly where her skirt starts.

"Here you go," Alexis speaks as she stands up from behind the desk. "That should keep you guys busy for a while."

"Thanks," Chloe responds, also standing, as much for Zach's benefit as for her own. She pulls her skirt back down over her firm thighs, giving Zach one last look, and then walks towards the door where Alexis is standing with a clipboard. She looks like someone with urgent business to attend to that doesn't involve Chloe, so Chloe just takes the clipboard from her, thank her, and exits the room. She hears the door shut behind her but doesn't look back, looking instead at the neat handwriting on the top page.

"Don't even think about it Zach, you know company policy!" Alexis's tone is stern.

"What? Chloe? Never. But a guy can look, and she is easy to look at!" Zach's response is too casual for her, almost as though what he was actually saying was 'given half the chance I would hump her every way into Sunday.'

"I'm serious Zach, not unless you want me to have you

replaced?" Again Alexis is stern, needing to make a point but having no intention of having the young Zach replaced. She's just gotten used to him, and the thought of going through the motions with a new intern would be more of a distraction than she can stand right now.

"Me too..." Zach really sounds more and more like he would rip Chloe's clothing off in a heartbeat.

Chloe goes down the list of things in her hand, not really reading it. She is looking for something. But it's not there. Why has Alexis left the plaque off the list? Perhaps she herself wants to investigate it. She goes through the items on the list, immediately ticking off in her head the things she doesn't want to do. And by the time she is in the open-plan again the research items that she would personally like to do are on the tip of her tongue. Nobody argues with her.

Alexis has to wait until 5 PM to get some alone time in the lab. The researchers are a diligent bunch, but not so diligent as to stay after hours. Or maybe it's because nothing on the list excites them enough to work until 9 PM, by which time all archeological staff is required to leave the building.

She carefully removes the plaque from its casing and gives it a long hard look. She makes notes, and sketches, trying to figure out what manner of destruction will befall the world next year. 3000...3000...three thousand. What if it's not even a year? But if not, then what? What could it be?

The room lights up, a luminous red, and she knows it's time to go. She packs her notes into her handbag after returning the plaque to its casing. She will have to continue her work at home, with no chance of completing it at the lab, at least not until tomorrow.

The whole area that she walks through is flashing now, and she quickens her step. She wonders for a moment what it would mean for her if she stayed until five past nine. But she keeps on moving forward, through the security checkpoints until she has exited the building. Everything seems to work faster too, particularly the elevators, and by 9 she is standing outside in the rain waiting for her cab.

She works until well after midnight back at her apartment. The time seems to fly by, and she is anxious. Sleep doesn't come easy when she eventually gets to bed, and she tosses and turns until her alarm goes off. But she is determined to make sense of it all before she has to stand in front of her bosses and present her progress to them. The day of the report comes too soon.

"Ah, Alexis, come in my dear." Grant is wearing a t-shirt and shorts, flip flops seal the look. He is seated in the massive boardroom. It's just him and Alexis in the room, everybody else joining in via satellite; their images will come into focus on several screens around the room in a minute. But Grant wants a chance to speak with her first, to make sure that they're on the same page.

"Mr. Chambers." She greets him, formally, and then takes a seat near a computer that is connected to a large projector screen at the far end of the room. Grant looks at her curiously, as if he knows that she is hiding something but he doesn't quite know what. She just pulls her skirt over her knees, her flash drive in hand, ready to begin. She too is looking at him, but simply because he is the only other person in the room and for her to look anywhere else would be rude.

The screens light up, and Alexis braces herself, almost as if the faces on the screens around her were in the room. She plugs her flash drive into the side of the laptop and waits. The pleasantries around her offer little by way of distraction as she sets up for her PowerPoint presentation.

She is calm and measured. As the slides appear on the screen behind her, she offers up explanations of their origins. She is careful not to give up anything that she has been working on, but the room is tense as if they are expecting more from her. By the time she gets to the last slide and opens the floor for questions, there is a deathly silence. The faces on the screens look at other faces on other screens and Alexis feels like they are all in one room, in a distant place, or perhaps even in the building.

A slow applause comes from China, followed quickly by Brazil. Then they all clap, thanking her for her good work and encouraging her in her endeavors. She can't help but sense relief. This bothers her but she is not in a position yet to let it be discovered. So she just thanks everyone, and then the screens fade to black.

"Very good my dear," Grant says, standing as she pulls her flash from the socket. He walks her to the door. Only then does she notice that he has shorts on, and she wonders if the world hasn't perhaps gone to the dogs; well at least to the hippies. She also realizes that the boardroom was cold, very cold, too cold for the people's president to be wearing shorts.

She takes the afternoon off, as she usually does after she has presented to the world essentially. This is just her second briefing but she feels like she's done a million of these presentations. She doesn't need the afternoon off either, but Grant insists and so she does.

Alexis thinks of the past couple of months that she has headed the division, she wonders what it is about Grant that unsettles her, aside from his 'my dears'. She wonders why they don't have a scheduled de-briefing, as they do with the other departments. She is just told the day before that she is going to brief the entire world on the progress she is making, and then afterward the entire division is given the afternoon off. She tries not to let the seeming haphazardness get to her, but it does. It is as if nobody really takes her department seriously; all the more reason to keep her findings to herself until she is sure. The last thing she needs is to embarrass herself in front of the whole world.

Chloe solidifies her plan to get inside the filing cabinet the following week. With no make-up on, she puts her hair in a neat ponytail to expose her fine cheekbones. She wears a tight top and an almost-too-short pencil skirt. Her heels give her extra height so that her legs gain an extra mile. She leaves her white lab coat hanging over the back of her chair for the first time during the day and makes her way down to Alexis's office.

She knocks on the door, waits to be acknowledged, and then steps into the office with a confident strut. She knows what she's doing, and she hopes that the young Zach will fall for it. She knows he will.

Once inside the office, she turns her attention to Alexis, and goes through the list in her hand, updating Alexis on their progress. It's an unnecessary exercise, but one that she carries out with the sole purpose of being in this room, with Zach. She just needs to find a suitable moment to slip him the note in her other hand, neatly folded.

Suddenly Zach gets up, no longer able to contain himself so that he needs to create space between him and Chloe. He senses that this skirt is for his benefit, but he also can't help but think that she is just playing with him.

Chloe gets through the list quickly now, needing to get Zach alone for a moment outside. But he is gone too quickly, and the moment is lost. She needs to think of another plan.

She delays in the office now, watching the door, which is open. As soon as he reappears in the hall she will leave, and slip the note into his jacket pocket. Thank goodness Zach seems to think that the white lab coat is a prerequisite for his job.

It takes him a good ten minutes, which feels like an hour to Chloe since she has to make idle chit-chat with her arch-nemesis. But he finally comes strolling down the hall, surprised that she is still standing in the doorway when he returns. Chloe excuses herself and heads out in Zach's general direction.

"Hi Zach!" she says casually, emphasizing his name so that it sounds like she's called him anything but.

"Uhm...hello" Zach stumbles, not sure if he should stop and engage with her. Not sure if that is what she wants.

Chloe throws her eyes towards the open office door and sees nobody. Alexis must be sitting behind her desk working. She pulls Zach to her gently by his arm, careful about the cameras mounted everywhere so that you didn't know what the people watching them were looking at any given time. Zach comes easily despite wanting to run and hide in the bathroom again.

She drops the note into his pocket quickly, and then she shakes his hand like they've never met before. Essentially they haven't, but they've seen enough of each other for this to seem odd, even to Zach. Chloe turns into the hall and walks with a strut that holds Zach's attention until she is out of sight.

He puts his hand in his pocket and feels the note. He wasn't imagining things. He wants to take it out and read it but there is a lump in his throat that seems to have paralyzed his fingers.

.   .   .

Leaving the note where it is, he walks back into the office, completely flushed. He blushes through his handsome, unkempt face. Apparently, the young Zach also thinks that shaving would somehow diminish him as an archeologist.

He loses himself in the day's administration, trying in vain to forget the little piece of paper in his coat pocket. By 5 PM he is unable to contain himself anymore. Zach usually is out of here by 1, but he had nothing else on so he stayed. He packs up his stuff, empties the contents of his pockets into his backpack, and heads out of the building.

He waits until he has cleared the last checkpoint before he turns to his bag and fumbles inside it for the note. It's still neatly folded and so he hesitates. Then he unfolds it, anxiety filtering through him like a million butterflies.

The handwriting is neat so that it would be impossible for him to misunderstand. But the words take a second to come into focus: Chloe, Call Me! There is a number too, and Zach's heart skips a beat. This is too good to be true, and so he thinks that she is definitely playing with him.

He walks a couple of blocks without realizing it, the note on his mind. When he finally hails a cab, it's almost 7. He wonders if he should try the number when he gets home. But his thoughts quickly shift to what's for dinner, and the note, although not completely forgotten, is put aside for the moment.

. . .

It's almost midnight when he thinks he should call, just to check that the number is listed. But what if she answers, what will he say to her? Why would he be calling her so late? It is Friday, and perhaps she's out. But he decides not to risk it, just in case she was home and she did answer. Hanging up would be juvenile, and this is no time to be juvenile.

The next morning Zach decides to wait until 10 to call her. If she answers, he'll play it cool. He can do this. After all, this is what he has wanted since he first saw Chloe. But why would she be interested in him?

He goes to his bathroom and looks at his reflection before making the call. He is very good-looking. He's been told this enough times for him to know that it's true. So why is he doubting himself now? Chloe just seemed so far out of his league that when she slipped him the note, he couldn't help but feel like he was being 'pranked'. In fact, even now as he dials the number, he looks around to see that there are no hidden cameras in his apartment, just waiting to catch his humiliation.

"Hello," Chloe sounds like she's been running.

"Hi, Chloe?" Zach knows that it's her as soon as she's answered. Relieved, the nerves come over him quickly so that he has to breathe deep.

. . .

"Zach?" She is as casual as though she had been expecting the call.

"Uhm, yeah. It's me. How are you?" He tries hard to steady himself so that the shaking in his belly doesn't flow up to his mouth and render the words inaudible.

"Better now. How are you?" She is really playing this very cool.

"I'm good. So, what's this about?" Zach tries to be professional, just in case he has this whole thing wrong, and it's not him she actually wants.

"Oh, I think you know Zach..." She lets the words settle on him.

"Oh?" Zach needs her to say it, to confirm what he hopes in his depths to be true.

"Come on Zach, this is no time to be shy. I know it's risky, but technically, you're not an employee of the World Government. So it's not like we'd be breaking any rules..." This is the confirmation he needs. Even the way she says it is leading like he is being led down a chocolate labyrinth to the creamy milky center where all his dreams will come true.

. . .

"Okay...so when do I see you?" Zach can't control himself, needing to know as soon as possible if it's just going to be sex, or if perhaps Chloe wants more. Somehow he knows that it will just be sex. But he's not complaining.

"Tonight?"

"Tonight it is!"

CHAPTER 3

GRANT CHAMBERS WANTS to see Alexis. The note on her desk lets her know as much, and since it's Tuesday, she is alone in her office. It's typed and on an official letterhead, so Alexis assumes that it is serious. But what could they possibly want to see her about, unless they've been perusing her filing cabinets, or the lab, in which case they will know that there's something she's not telling.

She is alone in the office, so she shuts the door, locking it automatically. She is nervous as she gets to the elevator, her finger suddenly allowing her access to the penthouse office suite. Her finger shouldn't work for this floor unless she is presenting to the world's leaders. But today it works, and soon she is inside the elevator headed for the top floor.

The elevator opens up directly into Grant's office. This is strange since anybody with a vendetta could just ride up the elevator and have direct access to him. But he wears shorts to board meetings, so Alexis dismisses this as just another one of his quirks. Perhaps he is trying to be as accessible as possible.

"Come in my dear, come in!" he says as the door slides

open. She steps into the space, surprisingly warmly furnished. The only other times she has been on this floor is to go into the boardroom, the elevator door only opening up to the side. It's cold as if the air-conditioning has gone on the blink. But Grant looks very comfortable and so Alexis says nothing.

"You asked to see me, sir," she states the obvious.

"Yes, come in, sit, drink?" He offers her a drink while pouring it, and hands it to her before she has a chance to turn down the single malt.

"Should I be drinking? I mean, I've got to get back to work!" Again she states the obvious in a painfully obvious way. But she is practically freezing now and her filters have gone.

"Just one, to warm you up my dear, go ahead. I'll have one with you if it would make you feel better." He pours himself a drink without waiting for her to answer and then goes in to toast nothing in particular. At least Grant is aware that his office is very cold, and at least he is trying to make her as comfortable as possible.

"What's this about sir, if I may?" Alexis asks the question before she sips the liquid that does an exceptional job of warming her from the inside. She still wishes that she had put on her lab coat though.

"That's the trouble with young people today, always in a hurry. Or they think they've done something wrong. You haven't done anything wrong have you, my dear?" He asks this as though he were telling her that she had, and for a second she doesn't know how to answer him.

"No sir, of course not," Alexis defends.

"Good...good. Nothing serious, yet. It's just that we've received another shipment of artifacts that it would be impossible to house here. So there you go..." He hands her a set of keys and watches her as she looks down at the set. He passes the time by sniffing the scotch without drinking it.

"And these?"

"These, my dear, are keys!" he states, matter-of-factly.

"For?" Alexis asks him, trying to be as matter-of-factly as him.

"They're for a storage facility, not too far from here. You see, my dear, there's been a shipment of artifacts that we think you should take a look at. But we don't have the facility to house these here. Will you go and take a look?"

"Yes, sure. When?"

"At your earliest convenience, my dear. Your earliest convenience would be fine."

She waits for him to mention the plaque, but he doesn't. Instead, he pours her another drink, the one in her hand barely finished. She takes it, the coldness of the room overcoming her again. But already she is feeling light-headed. Alexis notices how he doesn't drink; simply breathing in the aroma of the scotch. She is careful to sip this one slowly; very slowly.

She looks around the office, her eye falling on things that seem out of place in a president's office. There are three lounging areas, elaborately furnished. Behind his large desk is a steel chair, a throne of sorts that seems to come from another time and place. There is a bookshelf with rows and rows of books. But they're all the same book, Stephen King's The Tommy Knockers. This is odd décor she thinks to herself, especially for a room so cold. There are several fireplaces, she counts eight. But not one of them has a fire going despite the cold.

Alexis excuses herself, suddenly feeling very uncomfortable. She just wants to get out of this shrine to Stephan King. But Grant isn't ready for her to leave yet. He just looks at her for a long time before offering her a seat in one of the lounges. She realizes that she has no choice but to oblige him, and so she sits.

"You must find your work terribly interesting my dear." He sounds like he is asking a question and making a statement all at once.

"Yes sir, very interesting indeed."

"And you will be sure to report anything unusual to me should you come across it?"

"Yes, of course!" She senses that he knows that already she is hiding something, but that he doesn't want to scare her.

"Good, very good, my dear." She hates his use of 'my dear'.

"So why exactly did you give up your position as head of archeology, if I may?" She is trying for light conversation with a not-so-light question.

"I just needed to take a break from it all. It all became too much for me, my dear, as you will soon no doubt find out for yourself." This sounds almost threatening, sinister.

"No more stressful than running the world, I would imagine." She ventures on into a conversation that she would really rather not be having.

"I have an entire team to help me run *this* world. In archeology, you're pretty much on your own. And all the information gets to you eventually. I know it got to me. So now I just sort of oversee the running of things, but the decision-making is not mine alone, so there is far less pressure to be right. Do you understand what I'm saying, my dear?" He sounds like he's speaking to a five-year-old. Alexis hates this as much as she hates his 'my dears', and almost as much as she hates it when people call her Alex.

"I see," is all she can manage. Then she steadies herself

against the effects of the scotch and lets the last bit glide smoothly down her throat. It really is an exceptional scotch, which is why it is so strange that Grant doesn't once sip his, simply seeming to enjoy the smell of it.

She puts down her glass and gets up. She excuses herself again and this time Grant lets her leave.

"You will let me know if you find anything interesting in the storage facility won't you, my dear."

"Of course sir, you will be the first to know!" She reassures him.

In the elevator down to the basement, it feels like she has just come out of a dream. A haze lifts around her and she has to shake it from her like an oversized coat. When the doors open, she hurries out, needing the safety of her office for a reason that she cannot explain. Grant just seems to weave a charm around you that holds on tight unless you deliberately try to rid yourself of it. And even then, it tugs on your subconscious, like a puppet-master pulling the many strings of your psyche.

She falls on the sofa in her office and without meaning to fall asleep. She sleeps so deeply that only the red glow of the lights and the sound of the alarm pull her from her sleep. She has to hurry out of the building, almost gliding through the checkpoints. But she places her finger perfectly on the scanner each time and manages to keep her eyes open without blinking so that the retinal scan can be carried out without a glitch. Soon enough she is free from the building, and the seeming hold that Grant Chambers had on her.

She decides that Monday would be the best day for her to check out the facility. Zach is back at headquarters, going through the motions of admin, and the research team is sufficiently occupied with what she has given them to do. She arrives at the address Grant gave her, finding it easily.

She soon realizes why she has so many keys. There are nine bunkers to get through.

After going through a security checkpoint, surprisingly just one, she is on the massive lot that houses the bunkers. She goes to the first one, tries the first key on her bunch and the lock gives way easily. Alexis wonders why these artifacts don't have as much security as her weekly shipments, but then she assumes that they are probably just trinkets from times gone by, so one security checkpoint would suffice. Besides, who would be interested in ancient artifacts, since nobody can own them outside of the World Government, and so they don't fetch any sort of price on the black market.

Rows and rows of shelves as high as the ceiling are neatly packed with boxes. She chooses one at random and opens it. It contains burial masks, probably Egyptian, neatly enclosed in bubble wrap. She removes one and looks at it, straining in the dark to see the intricacies of its design. She looks for a light switch and finds it near the door. Suddenly the room is washed in white light and it takes her a while to adjust.

She returns to the box she's already opened and takes out the rest of the masks. All of them are similar, and all of them are authentic. She would have loved to have been a part of the dig that unearthed these treasures. She can just imagine the excitement on-site, probably deep within a pyramid, where these were found. She gets a chill of excitement down her spine.

She carefully wraps them again and returns them to the box. She realizes that her chill might equally have come from the room, which is very cold. But that is to be expected, given the contents of the bunker. She moves on to the next box, a nervous excitement as she lifts the lid off of it.

Inside she finds more masks, but not burial, more like warrior masks. She can't be sure so she takes out her notebook and scribbles notes on it, their design, every detail that she can think to record. Her excitement now comes over her in waves, as she realizes that each piece in this box too is authentic. Where on earth did they uncover this? She tries to place them at a specific period but can't, so she just makes more notes.

She gets through half the rows in the first bunker before she looks at her watch. It's 11 PM. But she isn't tired, feeling like she can go on forever, each box that she opens holding secrets from long ago, secrets that she wants to uncover. But common sense prevails and she closes the box. She will return again on Wednesday to continue with her perusal. She isn't looking for anything specific, merely excited by what each box contains, and the story it tells.

She waves at the security guards at the gate. It's a different set of men, probably due to a shift change, but nonetheless, they wave her courteously through to the cab that is waiting for her on the other side. For a moment she thinks she hasn't locked up properly, not understanding why these bunkers have such an ancient lock and key system. The World Government probably didn't want to spend any money on a fancy biometric system, just in case, Alexis is not the only person who might have access to these treasures.

Alexis does come back on Wednesday, and then Friday after she is done cataloging the shipment she received at headquarters. She works through each box systematically now, making notes, not trying to figure anything out, just making notes on the contents and basic descriptions. She numbers each box for ease of reference when she wants to return to it.

It takes her three weeks to get through all nine bunkers, and by this time she is as excited as a child who has just been handed the keys to Disneyland. She has hundreds of pages of notes by the time she is done. As she pages through them she gets more and more excited, not sure why. But something starts to tug at her gently like the reigns on a horse in a gentle gallop. She is being pulled in a certain direction by all this information, and she starts to understand what Grant meant when he said that it all just became too much for him.

Now she has to go back to the beginning, analyzing each and every piece, trying to find its place in the bigger picture. But she also needs to create a distance between herself and this monumental task. She might even need help. But from whom? Who can she trust not to go blabbing to the president every time they make a new discovery? Alexis feels it in her gut that she might be on the verge of something big, and she doesn't want to be interrupted until she is sure of the facts.

She juggles her duties at the World Government with her new obsession with the bunkers and their contents. But it is a stressful juggle. Every time she is at headquarters she just wants to be at the bunkers, and every time she is at the bunkers time seems to fly by and she doesn't seem to get much done. But one person is very happy that she is out of the office so much. And she takes full advantage of the time she has alone with Zach, luring him deeper and deeper into her web until he will do almost anything for her.

Chloe and Zach have been seeing each other for about three weeks now, and it hasn't been an uneventful time. He's not half bad in bed, and Chloe actually enjoys their trysts. But she needs to stay focused, and now that it seems that Alexis is out of the office on Mondays, Wednesdays, and Fridays, these are her best days to get into Alexis's filing cabinet, when Zach is alone in the office.

Chloe decides to broach the subject of the filing cabinet after a rather eventful Saturday of lovemaking. Zach is lying naked on her bed, the sheets a mess, the pillows on the floor. Like Samson, he is weakest after he has made love, both in body and in mind. Still, Chloe is careful in her approach.

"So, Alexis seems to be out of the office a lot lately. Any idea why?" She asks this while straddling his sexy frame. Immediately Zach responds to the joys of youth. She grinds against his manhood, hardening already with every movement.

"Something about a special consignment, I'm not sure myself, she's very hush-hush about it." He brings himself up to sitting so that he can kiss her. She lets him. As they kiss he manages to maneuver them so that now he is on top of her. He wants her again, despite them already having made love three times.

"Special consignment? That sounds rather ominous. You sure she isn't just bunking work to get her nails done? And leaving you to do all the mundane admin?" Zach has already positioned himself on top of Chloe so that he can move into her in a single stroke.

"She mentioned something about bunkers not too far from headquarters. And that she might be on to the discovery of a lifetime." He proceeds to mount her with great care, making sure that this is what she wants. She looks like she wants it. She moans like she wants it. So they continue the conversation while Zach extracts as much pleasure from Chloe as he is sure now he is giving her.

"And she keeps it all on file?" She asks, adjusting herself underneath him so that he can move easily in and out of her.

"She keeps everything on file. She's a stickler for detail." Zach's responses are now made under his breath, as he carries himself closer and closer to the edge.

"In the office?" Chloe presses, needing to know.

"Yes, yes, yes!" Zach is answering her question as much as he is appreciating the moment.

"Do you think I might take a look when she isn't there of course?" Chloe needs him to answer now before he finishes and returns to his senses.

"Yeah, sure, anything...for...you!" Zach's response is emphatic as he reaches his climax and then brings Chloe to hers. He is anything but an incapable lover, but she needs to remain focused. She needs to keep her eyes on the prize.

"When?" she asks Zach as he finishes up on her.

"When what...oh...the filing cabinet...Monday?"

"Monday's good. Monday is very good indeed." She rolls out from underneath him and goes into the shower. Zach joins her, and before long they are making love again. She needs to keep naïve little Zach happy just until she has what she wants. And if she is going to get into those filing cabinets on Monday, it won't be for much longer. She might keep him on hand though, feeding him just enough of herself to keep him satisfied and coming back for more. She also needs to keep his loyalties with her, so that he doesn't even think of mentioning it to Alexis. But Zach wouldn't dare, already breaking the rules of the World Government every time they sleep together.

But come Monday, Alexis is sitting behind her desk. She has mounds and mounds of paperwork in front of her, a result of trying to collate all that she has cataloged in the bunkers. She has decided that this is the week where she will try and make sense of it all, and unfortunately for her, this is the week that the World government, Grant Chambers to be precise, has decided that she will need the help of a researcher.

Chloe is quick to volunteer for the position, a step up from analyzing ancient scrolls. Also, it will give her the opportunity to be inside the office when Alexis needs to go to the bathroom or take a private phone call outside.

Alexis hates not working alone. Not that she isn't a team player, but she just likes everyone on her team to know their place. Perhaps it's a side-effect of having been given so much power so young. But she sucks it up, knowing that Grant Chambers himself couldn't possibly know what he is doing, and so she just hopes that he will realize sooner rather than later that she works best on her own.

A desk and chair are brought into the office for Chloe. It's a spacious office, but still, Alexis feels like the walls are closing in on her. She also has to come up with something for Chloe to do soon.

Chloe sets herself up behind her desk, looking far more comfortable than she should. It's barely 9 o'clock but already Alexis wishes that this day was over. She tries to work through the mountain of papers in front of her quickly so that she can figure out the best use for her new research assistant. As if Zach wasn't bad enough, now she has to deal with another person in her space.

The sexual tension between Zach and Chloe is thick and hangs in the room like a heavy cloud. Alexis waits for Chloe to be out of the room before she faces Zach about policy.

"Well, technically, I don't work here!" is his casual response, and Alexis knows that he has already crossed the line with Chloe, probably more than once.

"That isn't exactly true Zach, and you know it! You should know better, should've known better. And now you two will be working together in the same office. Need I remind you that in here the walls have ears?" She says this while pointing to the camera's not so cleverly hidden in the ceiling.

"Surely you mean eyes?" Zach responds, really not seeing a problem.

"Just as long as this little fling of yours doesn't compromise your work or mine."

"That's all it is Alexis, so you really don't need to worry. We won't be compromising anything but each other, in the privacy of her apartment." He winks as he says this, giving away his naivety. He really doesn't take his job here very seriously, and why would he?

All he's done up until now is the admin that Alexis couldn't be bothered to do, so why not reward himself with a little bit of Chloe in the meantime, until she gets bored with him and moves on. He can't imagine himself ever becoming bored with her.

By noon Chloe has had more coffee than she's ever had at work, part boredom, part sucking up to Alexis, who is a coffeeholic. Zach just sits behind his desk trying not to be turned on by Chloe, so close, and yet, because of the cameras, out of his reach.

Even with Alexis out of the room they cannot touch each other. It's torture for the young Zach, Chloe just enjoying the attention. She pretends to put stuff into a file and puts it in the filing cabinet, lingering just long enough over the many folders so as not to raise suspicion. She hadn't counted on there being cameras in Alexis's office, but the World Government really has covered all its bases. She just has to be content with the occasional sneak peek. But that's all she needs to know that Alexis is busy with a project that nobody, not even her employers are aware of.

Alexis spends her days collating her information with the help of Chloe, who is proving to be quite useful. But after hours, she heads straight for the bunkers, alone. She examines and re-examines pieces that don't quite seem to fit any particular period, making notes. It becomes clear to her that the world, at various intervals in human history, seems to have leaped forward technologically, and then taken a few steps back. It seems like after each spike in technology, the whole world paused to catch its collective breath.

She seldom leaves the bunkers before midnight, and so she misses dinner a lot. But there is a 24-hour take-out spot a few blocks from her apartment building and so she just gets something there, usually a Thai chicken salad. Tonight is one of those nights, and with the weather acting up, she has the cab wait for her, meter running of course, and drop her right in front of her building.

As the elevator moves swiftly up to her floor she realizes that it must have been just such a 'special consignment' that sent Grant Chambers over the edge. She walks down the long corridor to her front door and struggles for a moment with the key before she realizes that she has the wrong bunch in her hand. Once inside, she starts eating even before she has kicked off her shoes.

She eats while running the bath that she already knows she will fall asleep in. She gets out of the bath when the cold water stirs her awake, despite the temptation to just let the hot water run for a bit. She needs to sleep, and for the first time since she started at the World Government, she turns off her 4:30 alarm.

From then on her days start at 6:30. It's winter, so it's still dark outside, but this is a more acceptable time to rise, given the snow falling outside. She throws a winter coat on and wraps it tightly around herself as she leaves her apartment. She gets to the foyer and waits until she sees her taxi pull up before she exits. Despite the weather, she is at the World Government's headquarters by 8.

She is surprised to see Zach here since it's Thursday, but one would think that she would be used of it by now since he came in whenever he had nothing else to do. Even the 'life' he so often reprimanded himself for not having was at headquarters now, in the form of the lovely Chloe.

Chloe walks into the office a few minutes after Alexis, not apologizing for being late because technically their day starts at 9. She takes off her coat to reveal a short skirt and leggings, probably for Zach's benefit. Alexis suddenly feels over-dressed in her jeans, but the weather outside renders Chloe's ensemble totally impractical. Not that she is in any way concerned with practicality when it comes to her wardrobe, just as long as it has the desired effect. And apart from the 'no makeup' rule, there is nothing in the regulations that says anything about what they can wear.

Again Zach cannot concentrate, and he wishes that he had stayed home today. But the thought of going all these hours without seeing Chloe is too much for him. He is hooked, badly. And even the torture of having her close enough so that he can smell her perfume, but just out of his reach because of the cameras is a better punishment than not seeing her at all. Again he lets Chloe get all the coffee, not able to move from his seat without giving away what's going on between his legs.

One thing is clear to Alexis now though, and that is that all is not as it seems in the world. She wonders how many people on the planet know what she's discovering. How many people are aware that we have, at times, been visited by intelligent life from other worlds? And could this life still be here on earth, walking amongst us, just waiting for an opportunity to turn on us and take over our little planet?

She groups all the artifacts that seem to have come from another time, everything that seems oddly placed in the pieces of the period. She notices one thing, one common thread amongst all of them. What we used as tools for agriculture and hunting, are actually weapons!

It can't be. Alexis works tirelessly now, trying to figure out what the next apocalypse might be, in less than 2 months, if the calendar is to be believed. But both previous predictions were on point, so why not this one?

She takes a risk, the first real risk she's taken since she started working at the World Government. She smuggles the second plaque out. Alexis manages this by concealing it in her coat, not very original, but it works.

She gets back to the bunkers just after 7 PM, picking up some dinner first. She hasn't eaten properly since she started working on this puzzle. And now that the fate of the world, or at least the world as she knows it, hangs in the balance, she needs to keep her wits about her.

At bunker number nine she sets up a makeshift lab. Using her credit card, she purchases some equipment, just the basics, but they will have to do. She needs to solve this puzzle. And she needs to solve it fast!

She looks at the pieces in front of her, from various boxes from each of the nine bunkers. Intricate weaponry in front of her, the calendar that ends abruptly at the year 3000, she wonders what this means.

She uses her personal laptop, researching the origins of each artifact, mostly Mayan and Chinese, some Greek, but one thing she is sure of is that they are weapons. What on earth would extra-terrestrial weapons be doing on earth? How did they get here? And is it possible that those who brought these weapons here are still amongst them? Nothing makes sense to her anymore.

She wants to tell Chloe, or Zach, just somebody so that she is sure she is not losing her mind. She locks up the bunker just before dawn and heads home to shower. She must be at the headquarters at 8 AM of this particular Friday, another presentation. What will she tell the world's leaders? How can she just walk in there and tell them that in a few months the world will be overtaken by aliens? It sounds absurd when she says it out loud, but what else could it all mean?

The boardroom is colder than usual, probably because of the falling snow outside. And there is definitely air-conditioning, and it definitely works, but why wouldn't Grant make use of it? Again he is wearing shorts as he greets her and Alexis can't help but think that he has lost his mind, or at least that he has a clear death wish.

"So, my dear, anything interesting in the bunkers?" he asks her before pressing the button that will turn on the screens around the room.

She thinks carefully, nothing prepared, not even her handy flash drive to stall. "Well, sir, yes actually. There seem to have been periods in our history where we made advances technologically, but then we dipped, and receded back to our primitive ways, almost as though the whole world collectively decided to catch its breath." She looks at him for a response, and when he doesn't respond, she knows that he wants her to continue. "I've found some burial masks, some warrior masks as well, and..."

"Yes, my dear?"

"I've uncovered what seem to be weapons, sir," she says before she can stop herself and because she has nothing else to say.

"Are you sure they're not just primitive tools my dear?"

"No sir, definitely not tools. And there's one more thing..." she thinks of the plaque.

"Yes, my dear?"

"Uhm," she stutters, not sure how to broach the matter of the calendar. At the last moment, she decides not to, needing a little more time to figure it out. "There are glaring gaps in our history, times where nothing seems to have been happening, or very little by way of progress. And then we spike again, progressing technologically, far more than we should given the periods that follow these spikes." She leaves it at that and reports the same to the World Government when the screens finally come on.

She can't wait to get out of the room, which has the tip of her nose icy because of the temperature. She excuses herself and heads straight out of the building, not even stopping at her office to check up on Chloe and Zach. Something isn't quite right. And she is running out of time to figure out what it is.

CHAPTER 4

DECEMBER COMES QUICKLY, and it is really literally pouring with snow outside. But the World Government isn't big on holidays so anybody who works there can basically work right through them. This is what Alexis does. She has a month to decipher the pattern once and for all, but she thinks she knows what is going on.

Chloe hovers over here now to the point that it becomes uncomfortable for her. It's the first week of December, a time when businesses are shutting up for the year, everyone going off to think about their sins and make plans for the turn of the century. But Chloe doesn't seem to have any such plans and so she works even more closely with Alexis now.

Alexis comes in to the office very early on this particular Tuesday. She has her personal laptop with her, not doing anything that has to do with the plaque on the one she was assigned by headquarters. She knows she's probably just being paranoid. But Grant Chambers has been acting stranger and stranger over the last while so that she feels compelled to keep what she knows to herself for the time being. But she is running out of time.

She goes through the notes for the thousandth time, drinking her first cup of coffee at work. It's just after 6 AM. But her office is warm and so she chooses to work here, avoiding the rush of traffic slowed down by the snow. She looks up at the cameras often, too often, so that whoever is watching her knows that she knows that she is being watched. But she has never seen a speaker or anything resembling a bug in the office, so she assumes that they are watched just for the sake of, and to avoid any hanky panky between colleagues.

Chloe arrives just after seven and plants herself behind her desk. She has worked diligently on the assignments that Alexis has given her, and Alexis appreciates her enthusiasm. But having Chloe in such close proximity to her makes it awkward for her to work. Eventually, Alexis relents, calling Chloe over to her desk, showing her charts on her laptop that track human history, asking her advice. Before she knows it it's 5 PM and Chloe leaves, thankfully. Now Alexis can get on with the real work at hand.

As she gets on with the work, she realizes that she is getting closer and closer to figuring it out. The pieces that represent gaps in the history of human existence all fit together, perfectly. They tell a story of their own, a story that is not altogether human. She catches her breath many times in the hours that she spends at the bunkers, realizing that extra-terrestrials have visited our planet, at specific periods of seeming natural disasters, and realizing that some of them have probably remained behind.

But where are the extra-terrestrials now, and what have they come to do? This question bothers her. She researches UFO sightings over the millennia and researches the areas that have been claimed to house artifacts from outer space, but many of these have long since been abandoned.

She quizzes over this for a long time, and it's past midnight when she catches herself in thought. If she is right, then there will be another natural disaster in the year 3000, and aliens will again come to help us rebuild our world. But why? She takes this question home with her.

Once home she barely kicks off her shoes and opens up her laptop again. She just has to figure out what is going to happen at the turn of the century. She turns on her TV, just for background noise. Alexis finds the distraction forces her to focus on the work in front of her.

The screen lights up with preparations for the year 3000. Almost every channel has something or other at the turn of the century. All those people, jovially preparing for what could just be a catastrophic time. She remembers all the reports in the year 2000. It was years before she was even born, hundreds of years. But nothing happened. The disaster came in the year 2157.

She opens window after window on her computer screen. It was a flood. Worldwide. No pictures. Just archives of those who survived it. Nothing on how they survived it mind you, just sudden appearances of pockets of humanity on the first islands that reappeared after the disaster.

America is always the first to go, from what she can gather. New York was underwater in minutes. People battled to get to higher ground, the tops of buildings, the Statue of Liberty. She tries to put herself in their shoes, imagining the fear, the hopelessness. But then America was always the first to recover; the land of the free; the land of the damned.

Christmas comes and goes; and then New Year. She wonders if perhaps she has gotten it wrong. Or if perhaps the disaster will come years after she is gone. I mean, who can really accurately predict the future. They got it wrong in 2000. And now it seems they got it wrong in 3000. The Mayans seem to have been obsessed with the end of the world.

Alexis works throughout the holidays, no longer piecing together the history of mankind, but concentrating on the movement of extra-terrestrials amongst us. It makes for much more interesting work, but it falls just outside the ambit of her assignment with the World Government.

She collates the information regarding UFO sightings and landings. It would appear that the World Government went out of its way to cover these up. And if they put so much effort into covering it up, then there must be something to cover up. She must keep digging, searching. She keeps the calendar close at hand, looking at the end bit of it often. 3000. 3000. 3000. What if it isn't a year? But if not, then what could it be?

By the second week of the New Year, everything seems to have returned to normal at the World Government. Everything but Zach, whose desk is conspicuously empty. Alexis wonders where he could be before she realizes that he probably took a job on a dig site as soon as he graduated. She will miss him.

She will miss him even more now that Chloe seems to have taken up permanent residence at his desk. She wonders how long it will be before she has another assistant to handle the daily admin. But for now, Chloe is already more than she can handle.

"So I see Zach's gone," Chloe states the obvious, looking more comfortable than she should behind his desk.

"It was a temporary thing." Alexis wishes it was more permanent. Zach didn't speak as much as Chloe, and he definitely never felt the need to draw a conversation out of her at every turn.

"At least now we can see each other freely." Chloe hints at her affair with Zach, which is obviously still going on. The sex must be getting better and better.

"You were seeing one another?" Alexis asks what she already knows.

"Yeah, it was pretty casual at first. But I think I really like him, you know. Have you got somebody Alex, away from here, someone to get your mind off work?" Alexis really doesn't want to be having this conversation, and she definitely doesn't want to be having this conversation with Chloe.

"No!" Her answer is emphatic, almost as though she is putting a full stop to this conversation.

"That's a pity, you know what they say about all work and no play!" Chloe tries to feel her out, wanting more from her than Alexis is going to give up.

"...that it gets the job done?" Sarcasm is always Alexis's best defense.

"You're funny. I wonder..." Chloe says, looking away like she has an idea brewing in her head.

"What exactly is it that you're wondering Chloe?" Again she wishes that there was a shortening for her name that would make her sound like a man, but she comes up short.

"Just wondering..." Chloe responds although it is clear that she is processing all the information that she has gathered thus far about Alexis and trying to place her with some or other of her friends. "You're not lesbian are you Alex?" She asks this really wanting to know, not wanting to embarrass her brother when she finally hooks them up, which is her plan.

"I'm definitely not a lesbian Chloe," is her response, if you don't count that one time in college, she thinks, but doesn't say.

"Good!" And the conversation ends there.

"Chloe, you're late, again!" It's the same every week. Tucker leaves his third message on his sister's phone. She agreed to be on time tonight, it's Thursday, and apparently, she would be away for the weekend. Chloe listens to this message as she walks through the restaurant, Alexis in tow.

Now Alexis would not have accepted this invitation out, certainly not with Chloe, and definitely not, had she known that it was a setup. But she's already here, so she might as well suffer through it.

"You're relentless!" she says to him as he stands up, staring at her questioningly while kissing her on her cheek and pulling out a chair for her. He lets Alexis take his seat, and turns to pull a chair out from the next table. "This is Alex, we work together!" That's all she needs to say for Tucker to know that he is being set up on a blind date. Fortunately, Alexis looks as confused as he is.

"It's actually Alexis," she says, reaching for his hand, already extended.

"This is Tucker, my annoying older brother." Chloe almost sounds like she has a little more than an orchestrated affection for him.

"Hi, I'm Tucker." He introduces himself again, trying to catch himself but unable to avoid giving Alexis the once over. Even dressed for work he can tell that she works out, or that she has good genes.

"So, if you kids will excuse me, I just need to powder my nose." She gets up to leave without asking Alexis to accompany her.

"I'm sorry, I didn't know..." Alexis starts. She feels the incredible urge to explain herself, or at the very least explain away the embarrassment flushing over her like a shower.

"It's okay. My sister thinks I need to get a life. And I think she's tired of waiting for me to get said life. Actually, I think she just wants me to stay out of hers...so, anyway, I'm a detective. And you?" Tucker is struggling for conversation, not expecting this, and certainly not expecting Alexis to be so hot.

"I head up the archeological division at the World Government," she answers, with more pride than is necessary, but what the hell, she probably won't see him again.

"So you're Chloe's boss? She's ambitious! I wonder what she thought we'd have..." in common, is what he was going to say, but Chloe returns to the table, a waiter in tow, ready to take their order.

Alexis orders a double whisky, not needing to impress Tucker with her sobriety, and needing it if she is going to make it through this 'date'! Tucker orders the same, surprising Chloe since she is usually the one drinking at these weekly date nights. Tucker usually has a stakeout to get to directly after, but clearly not tonight.

The conversation is easy for the most part, especially since they have a guest, and so it is not necessary for them to broach the subject of their parents, the real reason for these dinners. Alexis and Tucker are politely cautious with one another, both of them wanting to get an opportunity to ask

Chloe what the hell she was thinking, but neither of them needing the bathroom yet.

Eventually, Alexis gets it out, no reason for pretense and certainly no need to ensure another date with Tucker. "So, Chloe, you never mentioned that you had a brother, or that we would be meeting him here tonight?" She actually needs to ensure Tucker that she knew nothing about this.

"Oh well, I just figured you're single, he's single, and we needed to eat. No harm done!" Chloe's response is cool as if there is nothing unusual about setting people up on a blind date without at least one of them being aware of it.

"I can eat at home!" she defends, not wanting Tucker to notice her noticing him, for the first time, the light in the restaurant playing up all his features.

"This is not a bad place to eat," Tucker interjects, feeling the distance that Alexis is trying to create between herself and the situation.

After a moment's silence, Alexis bursts out laughing. Tucker joins in soon after, unable, try as he might, to control himself. Chloe looks from her brother to Alexis and back again, and when it seems that they will not stop laughing, she gets up, takes her purse and her coat, and leaves the restaurant before their dessert gets to the table.

Alexis and Tucker share her mousse while making fun of Chloe in her absence. Alexis really didn't want to come to dinner with Chloe, let alone be set up with her older brother. But it hasn't turned out so bad. And after Tucker drops her at home, she finds herself thinking of him more than she should.

The next day Alexis can't wait to get to the office. She has a bone to pick with Chloe. But she decides not to be too hard on her, since she ended up having a very good time.

"Where did you go last night?" she asks, feigning concern.

"Oh, you two seemed like you were getting on, and I had another date to get to." Chloe lies unnecessarily. She went straight home and tucked herself into bed with a tub of Haagen Daz ice cream. It's become a ritual for her after her dates with her brother, just so that she can think of her parents in peace. It would help a hell of a lot if her brother wasn't the splitting image of their father. But he is, and it is what it is.

"So what was that exactly, and now wouldn't be a good time to lie to me Chloe," Alexis says, but her smile takes the edge off her words.

"Like I said last night, you're single, and my brother's single..."

"So you thought what?"

"I just thought that two single people might have a nice dinner on a chilly January night in New York City, that's all."

"That's all, huh?"

"That's all!" and Chloe leaves the conversation, and the room, needing to get away from Alexis before the obvious butterflies in Alexis's stomach make her vomit. She would rather her brother met another nice girl, any girl, just as long as it wasn't Alexis. But she needs to create just enough of a distraction for Alexis to allow her to get into the filing cabinet, and into her seat!

By the time she returns Tucker has already asked Alexis to lunch. Chloe hadn't expected this, but clearly, her brother still has some game. Alexis though doesn't seem to be too excited by the date, saying something about just being courteous since Chloe felt the need to let her brother have Alexis's number. At least she'll be out of the office for an hour, giving Chloe the time she needs to go through the file she so desperately wants to see.

But Alexis is having none of it. She locks up the filing cabinet and puts the key in the coat she throws on. Chloe watches her, faking a smile as she mumbles 'enjoy' to Alexis's back.

Tucker and Alexis don't stray too far from the headquarters, Alexis feeling the need to be close to the building. This is the first time she has actually gone out for lunch, and what would it hurt, she and Tucker got along very well the night before, and he probably just wants a chance to apologize for his sister.

"I'm sorry, about Chloe," he stutters as they make their way inside the coffee shop.

"No need to apologize, really, I had a good time!" she reassures him.

"Yeah?! Me too, but still, sorry." They leave it at that and proceed with the formalities of getting to know one another in an environment that wasn't orchestrated by Chloe.

. . .

"So, will you see him again?" Chloe fishes.

"I don't know...maybe!" is all she gets from Alexis, and they proceed with the work that Chloe could really handle on her own, Alexis's mind still on the bunkers.

When Alexis returns from lunch Chloe has her eye on her coat. She watches her take it off, and instead of using the coat hanger in the room, she lets the coat hang behind her massive chair. Then, after exchanging a few pleasantries that have nothing to do with the date she just comes from, Alexis leaves the room.

Chloe can't believe her luck. Yes, the World Government is probably watching her, but so what? It's now or never. She can't let this opportunity slip by.

She leans over her chair and watches Alexis disappear down the short hallway. She's probably going to the bathroom, so Chloe really doesn't have much time. She makes a dash for the coat.

After searching for a short while she feels what she is searching for. There's no time for her to bask in her glory, or worry too much about the eyes on her, she walks over to the filing cabinet. The first key fits the slot perfectly. She is almost beside herself with excitement.

She turns the key, once, twice, then the mechanism gives way and she is inside. She looks at the files, rows, and rows of folders in alphabetical order. Alexis really is very methodical. Or maybe it was Zach, who cares? She skims the front of a few files, nothing interesting.

. . .

Then she spots it. Tucked neatly after Z is a file marked Miscellaneous. She removes it quickly, taking her cell phone out of her pocket at the same time. She starts to take pictures, page after page, with no time to read it. She will have plenty of time for that later. She tries to go as quickly as possible, getting up to check the hallway once. Still no sign of Alexis, she returns to her espionage.

She gets about a quarter ways through the file before she catches herself. Alexis will come into the office at any moment now, so she knows that she won't get much more. She returns the pages to the file and returns the file into the slot she retrieved it from, the spot just after Z. She locks the filing cabinet and returns the key to the coat, not caring too much for which pocket she puts it in. She is seated back behind her desk by the time Alexis returns.

Chloe cannot contain herself so excited to get to the bottom of what Alexis has been researching, she pretends to have a headache as soon as Alexis is settled back in the office. Alexis offers her some water, not that she wants the headache to particularly go away. If Chloe leaves the office early, then she can get back to her research. But she doesn't want to come across as too enthusiastic.

"How are you feeling now?" Alexis asks after Chloe has half-drunk her water.

"I haven't had one of these in a while; I had seriously thought that I was rid of the damn things..." Chloe creates a history of headaches that she never had, not wanting to seem too eager to go home for something that can be solved with a mere Aspirin.

"I think it's best if I call you a cab, you can go home and sleep it off." Alexis really is dying to get Chloe out of the office.

"I think you're right. I might as well since I'll be of no further use to you here like this." Both girls get exactly what they want.

No sooner has Chloe arrived home then she connects her phone to her laptop. She brings up the pictures that she took of the file, transferring each file to her machine. Once the transfer is done she gets comfortable and settles into an afternoon of riveting reading. She can't believe that Alexis has kept this to herself.

Meanwhile back at the office, Alexis pulls out the file marked Miscellaneous. She senses that somebody else has been in the filing cabinet, the file in its position after Z, but not quite the way she would have placed it there. She puts it down to exhaustion and removes the file. She lays the papers inside it on her desk in piles, still unable to shake the feeling that someone has gone through her work. She checks herself, remembering which pocket she put the key to the filing cabinet before lunch, and remembering which pocket she just took the key out of, the same pocket. She shrugs off the feeling that she has and focuses on the work in front of her.

Chloe sinks into her sofa, getting chills at the constant references to 3000 in the notes in front of her. She looks at the sketches of all the items marked as weapons in the slides in front of her and wonders what could be going on, what it all means. Then she gets to the last page, with more references to 3000, and notes about extra-terrestrial life still on earth, and again she shudders.

We have been looking to the skies for signs of life on other planets for the longest time, and now it seems that they have actually visited earth. She feels like she's in the middle of an old Steven Spielberg film, but knows that what she is seeing in front of her is very real indeed.

Chloe needs to get into that cabinet again, just one more time, but she will need a little more time to get all Alexis's research. She calls her brother.

"Hello Tucker, how are you?" She puts on her best 'I care for you' voice.

"Chloe? This is a surprise!" Tucker genuinely appreciates the call. He appreciates any show of affection from his hard sister.

"So, Alexis huh!?"

"Don't start Chloe, and yeah, Alexis! What about her?" It's just after eight in the evening and Tucker sounds like he's trying to be busy so that Chloe doesn't feel the urge to pursue this line of questioning. The truth is, he has just got home and the only thing on his mind is Alexis.

"Lunch? I hope it wasn't a one-off." She needs to get an idea of where her brother's head is at.

"I hope so too..." He cuts himself off before he says more than he should.

"So I was thinking, maybe on Saturday, you can take her to that little Thai place we used to love. I heard somewhere that she loves Thai food. And maybe the theatre afterward, I also heard somewhere that Alex absolutely loves the theatre, but that she seldom gets to go, you know, work and stuff, and the fact that she just never seems to find someone to go with." Chloe makes it sound like she has information on Alexis that nobody else has and that Tucker should appreciate this heads up.

"Since when are you so interested in my love life little sis?" Tucker tries to move the conversation along, appreciating the information though.

"I'm not, it's Alex's love life that I'm interested in, or rather the lack of it. So, you game?" She tries not to sound too enthusiastic, but almost can't help herself.

"Yeah, we'll see. So how are you?" Tucker finally sees a gap to turn the conversation around, succeeding.

Come Saturday Alexis has made significant progress. She has discovered that aliens have indeed visited the earth, and left behind weaponry, weaponry that humans have mistaken for tools. She has also discovered that these visits have happened immediately after natural disasters that affected the whole planet. Probably before too, but the after seems more relevant to her research.

But the numbers don't sink, they just don't link up. 1000, 2000, and now 3000, surely these are years. But nothing happened in those years that adversely affected humanity.

The last natural disaster was in 2157. She wonders if perhaps the calendars are off by 150 years or so, but the makers of these calendars seemed so sure.

What is the significance of these numbers? And what is the significance of America always being the first to recover? Perhaps these two facts are not even related. Perhaps it's just a coincidence that America always seems to rise first.

She's just about to leave for the bunkers when her cell rings. It's Tucker.

"So I was thinking..." he says even before he says 'hello'.

"Yes?" She breathes into the phone.

"We could have lunch and then catch a show on Broadway?" He tries to sound casual, almost expecting her to have something on.

"I hate the theatre." She has composed herself sufficiently not to be talked into doing something she does not want to do.

"Okay, a movie maybe, or just lunch..." Tucker stutters, quickly making a mental note to get Chloe for lying to him.

Alexis doesn't take much convincing. She has free run of the bunkers so even if she goes through later, or tomorrow. She really wants to see Tucker again, and twice in one week makes it seem like a little more than friendship already. Perhaps he just wants to get laid, but she won't complain, trying very hard to remember the last time she saw some action.

. . .

"Lunch, and then we'll see." Alexis changes three times before she exits her building, Tucker already waiting for her outside, standing under the awning with an umbrella. Strangely enough, it's raining in New York, but she doesn't give this too much thought, just feeling slightly over-dressed when she sees him in jeans.

Chloe has got to the office by then. She looks around for the keys, not finding them. She takes a chance and goes up to the guys at security, wondering if they have a spare set. They don't. She goes back down to the basement and looks around for something to pry open the lock. Already she is thinking up an explanation to offer to the people she knows are watching her through the cameras. It's Saturday, and her finger shouldn't have even gotten her in the building.

Then she remembers Alexis saying something about leaving work at work, and she goes through her drawers again. In the third one from the bottom, she finds the keys to the filing cabinet, and her heart skips a beat. They are near the back, explaining why she missed them the first time.

She goes to the door and shuts it. There is nobody in the basement, even the cleaning staff is off. Nobody seems to work when it is not necessary at the World Government. Still, she can't risk anything now, any more than she is already risking.

She takes out the file in question, and armed with her cell phone, she starts to take pictures of the pages from where she stopped the last time. She is careful to get the pics just right this time, and after checking that she has all the information, every note, every squiggle in the frame, she starts to take pictures of every remaining page in the file. Again she has no time to read the pages, but she catches glimpses of the notes, and again she gets excited. And nervous! Very, very nervous!

When she is done it is almost 9 PM, and just before the alarm goes off, signaling that anybody in the building who isn't Grant Chambers needs to get out, she replaces the pages in the file, puts it back in place, and returns the keys to the place in the third drawer from the bottom, down the left side of Alexis's desk.

CHAPTER 5

BY MONDAY CHLOE has a comprehensive report that she would like to deliver to Grant Chambers himself. She arrives at work a full hour before Alexis, and after establishing that Grant is in fact in the building, she makes arrangements to be allowed up to the penthouse office.

"Yes my dear, what is it?" Grant is his usual cool self, and despite the snow having all but melted outside now, his office is freezing. He also looks like he's spent the weekend here, his shorts wrinkled, and he missed a button on his shirt. Chloe looks around for signs of a lover but sees nothing. Everything in the office is in its place. Not that she's ever been up here, but she senses that it's been just so for a long, long time.

She shivers through her presentation of the facts, highlighting as she goes that Alexis didn't notify them, or anyone, of the discovery. Grant is collected, and aside from his appearance, he doesn't bat an eyelid. He knows though what Chloe is after, and once she is done with her presentation, he offers her a drink.

"But it's not even 8 AM yet sir?" Chloe objects.

"So? All these rules you have, they're rather silly, don't you think, my dear?" By 'you' she takes him to mean heterosexuals, and so she accepts his offer. He pours them both a drink and they sit down on one of the large leather sofas in the room. She sips slowly on her drink, appreciating the warming sensation it provides her inside. Grant just breathes in the aromas of his drink.

"What exactly would you like me to do with this information, my dear? After all, we gave her the very artifacts that she has used to come to the conclusions she has come to. And we've even given her the keys to several bunkers that have some of these artifacts, bunkers that she has exclusive access to I might add." Grant searches deep in Chloe's eyes to the point that she becomes uncomfortable.

"I just thought you needed to know what she's been up to, that is all." Chloe tries to come away from this encounter with a shred of her dignity intact.

"And what if, my dear, what if Alexis was merely waiting until she had all the facts in place before she bothered us with this information?" Still, Grant is searching for something deep in her eyes, and again she is uncomfortable, taking refuge in her drink.

"I hadn't thought of that," Chloe admits.

"But you have been thinking of what it must be like

behind her desk, to be in total control of the archeological division, right, my dear?"

"Uhm, well, I had wondered..." Chloe admits.

"Ah, now we get to the real reason why you're here. Surely you don't think that anything happens within these walls that we don't know about my dear, do you? Do you think that we haven't been watching Alexis since she started here? And do you think that we have not been watching you, closely, my dear?" Grant asks these questions without expecting Chloe to respond, just letting the questions hang around her like the apples on a tree.

She just sits there sipping the remainder of her drink, thinking on the questions that he is throwing at her, without feeling a real need to respond.

"Tell you what Chloe, why don't you just back off of Alexis, doing everything she asks you to do, nothing more, nothing less. However, my dear, keep your eye on her. And if, after she has gathered all her facts, she still doesn't bring it to us, we'll discuss her position here and your possible promotion." Grant says everything that Chloe wants to hear to assure her that he won't tell Alexis about this little meeting. After another drink, she leaves the penthouse, leaving her research, or rather, Alexis's research, for Grant to peruse at his own leisure.

Grant paces his office after Chloe leaves, glass in hand. He has a good mind of smashing it against the wall but thinks better of it. He hadn't expected Alexis to be so bright. He will have to keep a closer eye on her from now on.

. . .

Alexis meets Chloe in the elevator and it is obvious where she comes from. But she doesn't ask. She just greets her and puts her headphones on. Alexis knows that this is rude since they're the only two people in the elevator, but she is a little distracted so that she doesn't even care. Chloe lets Alexis exit the elevator first, and she retreats to the bathroom, not wanting to deal with the question that should be at the top of Alexis's mind.

But Alexis doesn't ask. Not even when they are alone in the office. She clearly has other things on her mind. Like the weekend, especially Saturday, and her date with Tucker. Chloe is Tucker's sister, but Alexis too is not about to be answering questions about their date, and certainly not from Chloe.

To their surprise, they are asked to leave for the afternoon, something about routine maintenance. Alexis has her suspicions though, but it would be impossible for her to leave with the file. It doesn't matter how long you've worked at the World Government, you are subject to the same security check as everyone else, and while frisking is an outdated practice, the x-ray scanners at each point will definitely pick up the bulk. She thinks of the time she got away with the plaque, but she leaves it and heads for the bunkers.

Chloe heads straight home, calling Zach on the way. She needs to know if Alexis mentioned anything to him, her recent discovery suddenly feeling like it doesn't carry sufficient weight with her leader. Zach is available, and by the time Chloe gets to her building he is waiting for her in the foyer.

"So how are things at the old WG?" He isn't really interested, already thinking up creative ways to get Chloe out of her clothing.

"Things are good. They're running routine mainte-nance today, hence the free afternoon. And you, I thought you'd be on some major dig by now, getting your hands dirty in some exotic mud pit, extracting remnants from our colorful past?" Chloe is also thinking, but her thoughts go beyond sex.

"Well, remind me to that Mr. Chambers..." Zach says as they enter her apartment. He locks behind them himself and takes a hold of Chloe around her waist, turning her to face him in the process, not feeling the need just yet to answer her question. He looks into her eyes for a second before closing his own and wrapping his lips over hers. She kisses him back easily, already feeling warm in the places she wants him to get to.

He wastes no time getting her naked. Then he stands over her and undresses himself, watching her closely, exam-ining every perfect inch of her. With both of them naked, nothing stands between them and two hours of beautiful sex. By the time he is done Chloe is satisfied. She doesn't need to say it, it's written all over her face.

"So, Alexis's research, did she ever tell you about it, or about what she was working on?" She knows that now is the time to get a straight answer out of him.

"Come to think of it, she never mentioned what she was working on, but in the last few weeks that I was there, she was very distracted by it, whatever *it* was. How is she by the way?" Zach knows nothing. Chloe accepts that he was just good for the sex. But if he starts to think of this as a relationship, then she will have to think of a very nice way of ending it.

Alexis is working in the ninth bunker. She has the nagging feeling that something is staring her right in the face but she just can't see it. But what? What could she be missing in the hundreds of pages of notes, or in the artifacts themselves?

She starts by placing the items in the periods they are supposedly from, and using them as the humans did, as farming instruments predominantly? It's clear they make more sense as weapons. But this begs the question, for what, an intergalactic war that hasn't happened yet? Because from what she can gather there has never been such a war in the history of mankind. And why then would they leave all these weapons here on earth, out in the open, if this war was still to come? Could the earth just be one massive store-house for the artillery of a species from outer space? That's absurd.

She toys around with the weapons, making more notes which she will later put into her laptop to create charts. But nothing is making sense to her suddenly, and she hates the feeling. She hates not knowing what is going on almost as much as she hates being called Alex.

She calls Tucker and asks him to meet her at the coffee shop around the corner from the World Government headquarters. She needs a distraction, and Tucker is proving to be a very handsome distraction. He also has a wicked sense of humor, which she loves, but this is certainly not a relationship, she tells herself. It's not even the beginning of one.

They are just two New Yorkers with a little bit of time on their hands.

When they get back to the World Government the next day it is clear that a little more than 'routine maintenance' was carried out. Alexis notices cameras where there weren't any. Obviously, they want everybody to know that they're watching. Everyone else seems oblivious to this, but it really gets to Alexis, like they're watching her. The truth is they are!

Alexis goes straight to the drawer with the keys and finds them in their place. She takes them out and goes to the filing cabinet to check on her files. Everything seems to be in order. She pulls out the file that is uppermost in her mind and checks through it. Everything seems to be where she left it.

She pulls it out and goes to her desk to look through it. To her surprise, Chloe just sits at her desk, engrossed in past catalogs, waiting for the day's orders. They sit working silently until lunch, not even coffee is exchanged between them. Chloe doesn't offer Alexis any when she goes to get some, and Alexis returns the favor. They're not even being deliberately catty with one another, just giving each other space. Chloe gives Alexis the space she needs, and also the space she's been told by Grant to give her. And what the president wants, the president gets.

Alexis works through lunch while Chloe goes out. If it's space that Alexis needs, it's space she will have. At least now she knows where the keys to the cabinet are, and she will find time to get back in there if she feels she needs to.

. . .

By Friday Alexis has had it. She feels like there are eyes on her everywhere. She actually can't wait to shake this building from her. She waits for Chloe to leave, and then she locks everything up nice and tight. Although, as she moves through the various security checkpoints a thought settles over her. If she's being watched so closely, and she knows in her gut that she is, there is nothing to stop her superiors from going into the office after she has left, and going through her files.

By the time she has cleared the last security checkpoint, she lets this go, and heads in the direction of the bunkers before changing her mind, hailing a cab and heading home. If they want to spy on her then let them. She will just say that she didn't have all the facts, which is why she didn't tell them what she was working on, should they ask her.

And by 'they' she knows she means Grant Chambers, who has been her only superior since she started here. Everyone else seems to have found other things to do with their time since her interview.

She wonders if she should call Tucker, but decides against it, thinking that he must be out with his sister, or on a stake-out. It turns out that he is doing neither, and her phone lights up, Tucker's name flashing on the screen.

"Alexis. Hello!" Tucker sounds much surer of himself tonight than he ever has.

"Hello Tucker, you good?" She is relieved at the sound of his voice, needing something from him that she can't yet articulate.

. . .

"Am I seeing you tonight?" He asks the question but makes it sound like a statement.

"I don't know, are you?" She is trying to be as cool and confident as he is, but she is sure that he can hear her heart beating through the phone.

"Yes I am, you're coming to my place, I'm cooking." Hearing him say it, she knows that he can probably cook.

"Okay, send me your address, then you don't have to drive all this way to pick me up."

"Cool, sending it through now. See you later!" He puts the phone down before she has a chance to ask what to bring.

She gets ready and heads out to Tucker's place, which turns out to be a sprawling mansion in Winchester. She rings the bell, surprised when Tucker answers. She tried the button written 'apartment' first, but when she got no answer, she tried the main house. The gate opens slowly and she walks up a driveway so long she wishes that she had asked the cab to wait.

Standing at the front door with a million questions on her mind, all of them centered on this house, she rings the bell. Tucker appears through the glass panels in the front door and then he opens up for her, letting her in just in time. It has started to rain outside. Spring was promising to be very wet this year.

"I'm confused?" she says as he takes her coat.

· · ·

"It was my parents' place, they're dead now, and Chloe couldn't bring herself to live in it." His explanation is far too candid for her to even attempt anything but acceptance of what he says, and moving the conversation along quickly. Although, why he and his sister don't just sell the place is a question that nags her for a while until she deliberately puts it on the back burner for a time in the future when she knows him better.

After dinner, Tucker takes Alexis on a tour of the house. It really is massive, and the tour takes longer than her feet can stand the heels she is in. She takes them off, letting them hang at her side as he describes each space that they move into.

"It really is very nice," Alexis says, Tucker, turning around to see that she has no shoes on. He motions for them to move into an upstairs living area with a beautiful view of the suburb. She curls up on the couch comfortably, almost too comfortable. Tucker loves how at home she looks in the space.

The house is clearly still serviced by servants, everything immaculate and in its place. Even the bar upstairs is full. Tucker must have given the servants the night off. And his parents must have been very wealthy. But Alexis senses that to ask him about his parents now would just open up a whole other kettle of fish.

"So, does Chloe ever talk about the office?" She chooses a sensible line of questioning.

"Never... She usually can't wait to be gone from the restaurant. So anything that would keep her there longer than she has to be is avoided I'm afraid. But she really likes her job, from what I can gather."

"Oh, and me, what has she said about me?" Alexis is going somewhere with this line of questioning, but it seems to be pulling her in a million different directions.

"Just that you're always busy, and that you don't socialize much." Tucker tries to come across as tongue in cheek when he says this, but it really is something that his sister had said.

"And I assume that you are her attempt at socializing me?" Alexis is suddenly serious, trying hard though to hide her offense.

"I think that what she thought was that we would screw each other's brains out on that first night and then lose each other's numbers. I don't know though which one of us looks like they need to get laid!" Humor, Tucker's saving grace.

Alexis laughs, gathering that if Chloe had mentioned anything about the office, Tucker wouldn't have felt the need to keep it from her. So they sip on their drinks, warmed by the roaring fire in the hearth, Alexis thinking of Tucker 'that way' for the first time.

Chloe spends her weekend working on the copied file. She sees what conclusions Alexis came to, or what conclusions she was approaching, and she tries for alternatives. She needs to prove to the leadership of the World Government that she would be a better candidate for the job.

· · ·

But try as she might, she comes up short. She is just a researcher, and her head doesn't work the way Alexis' does. So she just comes to the same conclusions that Alexis came to, and where Alexis is still working on stuff, she comes up short.

Alexis in the meantime is spending her Saturday at bunker nine. She must figure out what all the information she is gathering means, if not for herself, then for the people who will be alive on the earth by the time the next catastrophe hits.

She examines the calendar for the millionth time. It seems to say that the next catastrophe will be fire. But didn't the dinosaurs go out in a ball of flames, the earth hit by an asteroid? But that time was followed shortly by an ice age, so what could the possible link be between fire and ice. She shudders at the thought, although the bunker she's in is a degree warmer than it is outside.

The plaque ends abruptly with the Mayan reference to 3000. They are in the year 3000, so it can't be that the catastrophe will happen at the turn of the century, or it would have happened by now.

Then it hits her, like a ton of bricks in her chest. Weapons mean that an army was sent to earth. She gathers that the numbers, 1000, 2000, and now, 3000 must have been the number of soldiers sent. It has to be. And the weaponry must have stayed behind because these aliens didn't need to upgrade it, humans would simply use it as farming tools.

. . .

But why have they never seen a real extra-terrestrial she wonders, even she, head of the archeological division of the World Government, why would they keep this from her?

She returns the plaque to its casing and gets out of the bunker, not even checking that she has locked it properly. What if she is right, and there are about to be 3000 alien soldiers deployed to the earth? She walks through the only security checkpoint and away from the bunkers, needing the distance. She calls a cab once she can no longer see the bunkers. But she can't shake the feeling that she is being followed.

She wonders if she should call Tucker, thinking better of it. Seeing him four times in one week would be a bit much for the 'not-a-relationship' that they're in. Alexis has the cab circle her block twice, looking over her shoulder for suspicious activity. Nothing. Thank goodness this is a new cabby, so he doesn't know where she lives and therefore doesn't feel the need to ask her if everything is alright.

She goes to a busy restaurant about two blocks from her apartment and after tipping the cab driver far more than she should have, she runs inside, feeling very edgy and uncertain about herself. She finds a table for two where most of the patrons can see her, and orders a drink, just to steady her nerves.

She has two more drinks before she exhales. She takes a deep breath and goes to the bathroom, after ordering a steak salad. In the bathroom she finds herself checking for cameras, which is absurd. But if she is right, then is it really?

Alexis returns to her table looking a little better. The

alcohol has had time to settle in her and she appears calmer. But her eyes are on the door, for what, she doesn't even know. How can she go from feeling relatively safe in New York to feeling so vulnerable in a matter of minutes? But she just can't shake the feeling that somebody is watching her. When her salad arrives she orders the fourth drink.

After seven drinks and a steak salad, she is ready to go home. She's not drunk mind you, just less anxious about what might or might not be following her. But if she gets a glimpse of anyone out of the ordinary, than she is of the sense to run, or do some serious damage with her pepper spray. This is New York City, however, and everyone is their own version of strange.

She waits just inside the restaurant, at the end of the bar, for her cab. Yesterday she would have walked the two blocks, but something has definitely unsettled her tonight. Tonight she would take a cab around the corner to get the paper and some magazines if it wasn't on her way home, and she didn't convince the cab driver to stop for two minutes while she picked up the items, meter running, of course.

In ten minutes she is in her apartment. She closes the door, and for the first time, she can remember she latches it locked, turning the key at the same time. If someone is after her, then she definitely won't make it easy for them to get to her. She goes to her own version of a bar and pours herself a more comfortable drink since she's home. She doesn't turn the lights on, enough light streaming through the large windows from outside. New York is still famous for its lights.

Alexis takes her drink to the bath with her, sipping it as she fills the bath. She gets in, and wills the stresses of the day away. But they aren't going anywhere, and she starts often, feeling like she's being watched.

She gets out of the bath and wraps herself in a robe. She picks up her phone in the living room and again thinks of calling Tucker. But what would she tell him, that she thought she was being followed and so she went out and got drunk and now she wants a booty call. She puts the phone down and pours herself another drink. Sleep will definitely come quicker if she's drunk.

No sooner has she put her phone down and a hand covers her mouth. First, she thinks she is imagining it, but then she realizes that the smell of tobacco on the fingers over her mouth, just under her nose, is very real. She tries to scream but the hand is wrapped tight around her mouth with no sign of going anywhere.

"Stop your research...or else next time you'll get a whole lot more than a warning." The voice speaking into her ear is a loud whisper. She tries to process what he is saying. She gathers that she will survive this assault from his reference to 'next time.' Immediately she is calmer and stops struggling against the hand that is holding both of hers behind her back. He pushes her to the ground hard.

She falls, and stays down, not daring to look up. She hears the door open and then close, so he must have been in the apartment when she got home. But why on earth could her research be a threat to anybody? Even the World Government gets to decide what to do with the information she gives them, and very seldom does it amount to anything more than a 'very well done my dear' from Grant Chambers.

When she is certain that she is alone in the apartment she gets up and turns on the light. She goes to the door and latches it again, locking it, making sure that it is locked, and then making sure again. She walks through the entire apartment turning on lights and leaving them on. She checks closets, and happy that she is definitely alone in the apartment, she goes to bed. But not after she has poured herself another drink, everyone that she had before the incident having left her system briefly, probably the shock.

Alexis sits up in bed, the lights on. She turns the drink in her hand, wondering what that was all about. She must be getting close to something that somebody doesn't want to get out of. But what? And who? Definitely not the World Government, she thinks. But they're the only ones who have access to her research and who know what she is working on. Them, and Chloe. She is sure that Chloe knows more than she is letting on. But what would any of them gain from threatening her like this, in her own home? What is the point of threatening her when they could just call her up to the chilly penthouse office suite and put an end to her research? It doesn't make sense to her.

She struggles to sleep, so she pulls her laptop closer and opens up the transcribed notes. Whats and whys fill her head until she eventually gives up the question. She just goes through the work in front of her as objectively as possible. But nothing can distance her from the fact that she was just attacked in her own home, and she dials 911 about six times. But each time she hangs up before the receiver is picked up on the other end.

The sun finds her still awake, staring at her laptop screen, the machine now plugged into the wall to charge the battery. Only when the sun kisses her face and finds her eyes does she realize that it's the day and that she has been up all night. She goes to make coffee.

She thinks about the attack, or rather the warning she received. She can't imagine that her life is in danger, but it's something that she must now accept. She showers and throws on a tracksuit. Alexis thinks of going to the gym for the first time, just to be surrounded by people. But she just pours herself more coffee and sits on her sofa, watching the rain falling outside.

The day goes by with her just sitting there, drinking coffee. She can't even bring herself to make breakfast or lunch. But come dinner time she knows that she needs to eat. She contemplates ordering take-out, but she decides to go out. She almost wishes that when she returns, the stranger who was in her apartment will be there, so that she can ask him some of the questions that are now burning like a fire in her chest.

She goes to China Town, quite a distance from her home. It's always busy there, and so she will be safe, she thinks. She walks through the stalls in the streets and passes many restaurants, looking in the large windows to see families seated around large tables having dinner. She wishes that she could just be a part of one of them, but she has sacrificed her family and friends for her work at the World

Government. But what for? To be threatened in her own apartment for doing her job?

Finding a busy eatery with mostly singles she decides to go in, not wanting to feel out of place. She wonders about her life, and who would miss her if she actually did die. She is probably being irrational, but these are relevant questions, considering this new threat to her that wasn't there on Friday.

She enjoys her dinner, forgetting for a moment the threat to her. Chinese have a way of turning every meal into an occasion, and this place is no different. Each dish that is served up to her is a taste of China, authentic in every way, and she wonders why she hadn't come down to China Town more often to eat or just to experience the richness of the immigrants that it houses.

Alexis is pleased that China Town hasn't changed in 100 years, hell it hasn't changed in 1000, and she finds herself caught in the rain as she walks through the night market. All that talk of triads and crime in the area seems to be a gross misjudgment of these beautiful people. Surely there must be some underhanded activity that takes place here, probably happening right now, but she doesn't think about that, caught up in the nostalgia of the moment.

It's after midnight when she takes a cab home. But she finds herself in a parked cab outside Tucker's Winchester home. For an hour she just sits in the cab, the cabby not minding because his meter runs as long as she is sitting in his cab. But she rethinks this and goes home. It takes her half an hour to get out of the cab outside her building, and her heart beats erratically in the elevator.

She stands for a further ten minutes outside her front door, the key in the lock. Eventually, she turns it and goes inside. The lights are all still on from the night before, and after making sure that she is alone in the apartment she goes to turn every single one-off. She settles into a luxurious bath with a glass of wine. If they want her, then let them come. But she knows somehow that as long as she plays ball, she shouldn't have any problems. At least she hopes so.

It's almost 3 AM when she eventually gets out of the bath and goes to bed. She sleeps naked, needing somehow to feel vulnerable, hoping that this will exorcise her fears. Wrapped in the covers, she falls asleep, leaving her wine half finished, and with her mind racing. One thing is sure, and this can't be denied; her research has rattled someone, and this is someone that doesn't want to be messed with!

CHAPTER 6

ALEXIS DECIDES TO CALL TUCKER. She needs to run her current situation by someone in the know just so that she is sure she is not losing her mind.

"Hello Tucker," she makes the call at around 4 PM on Sunday afternoon.

"Hey, Alexis, I didn't expect to hear from you," he lies. He has been watching his phone all weekend.

"Can we meet?" She gets straight to the point.

"That sounds ominous, sure, where?" His heart now skips a beat, and he wonders what she might have to say to him.

"I don't know; can you come to my house?" She can't bring herself to leave her apartment again. Not that she's scared or anything, she just wants the comfort of familiarity.

"Sure, I'll be right there!" He hangs up the phone and checks himself in the mirror. He could do with a shave, but

Alexis sounded a bit off, so the sooner he gets to her the better.

By the time he arrives, she has pulled herself together enough to attempt a little makeup. She has also managed to get the place sort of clean and presentable, this being the first time that Tucker will be coming upstairs.

She lets him in and catches herself before she locks the door behind them. The thought of having Tucker here, in her space, makes her feel immediately safer. She offers him coffee so that he knows that this is serious and that it's not just a social call. He accepts, and soon they are sitting on the opposite ends of her tiny dining table, staring each other square in the face.

Alexis is the first to look away, not sure where to begin, or if she even wants to. She rehearsed it and rehearsed it over and over in her head, but now that Tucker is here, she suddenly doesn't know where to start.

"Someone broke in here on Saturday..." she starts, looking at him for a reaction.

"In here, how?" The question makes sense. It's an apartment block with surveillance cameras everywhere and where nobody gets passed the front desk without being seen by half a dozen people at least.

"I don't know. But he was here when I got home on Saturday night." The thought that someone was in her home angers her now. But this is no time for emotion. She just needs to get the story out.

"Are you okay...was anything taken?" The cop in Tucker comes to the fore.

"No, I'm fine, and nothing was taken. But he had a warning for me..." Again she looks away, not sure of what it will sound like when it actually comes out of her mouth.

"A warning? What for? Are you in some kind of trouble Alexis?" Again Tucker is being a cop.

"I think so..." Alexis answers only his last question.

"What's going on, talk to me..." Tucker softens somewhat, trying to make himself more accessible to her, for her, so that whatever it is, she feels that she can come to him with it. He wants her to come to him with anything.

"I've been working on some research at the World Government, and I think that someone isn't very happy with the progress I've made..."

"What research...? Am I allowed to ask?" He backtracks, not sure what World Government policy is on such things.

She tells him everything. Lying to Tucker is impossible. She feels like he will see right through her. She tells him about the bunkers and then gets her laptop. They go through the notes on it until she is sure that he knows what she is telling him.

"What are you saying Alexis that aliens are...?" Tucker starts the question but isn't given an opportunity to finish it.

"Yes, Tucker that's exactly what I'm saying. And now with this warning, it's clear that I'm onto something, something big, probably much bigger than the fact that aliens have visited us from time to time, and that they will probably visit us again very soon if they're not already here." She says everything in one long sentence before her filters render any of it too absurd to say. But she knows what she knows. And now Tucker knows it too.

Tucker gets up and walks to the window, trying to process everything he is hearing. Alexis goes to get more coffee, black this time, with a shot of whisky. She has said what she wanted to say, said what she needed to. So now she feels the need to reward herself for probably making herself look like a complete idiot in front of Tucker.

He takes the cup from her, the whisky reaching his nose long before the coffee does. He smiles and takes a huge sip. He needs it as much as she does, albeit for very different reasons.

Tucker turns to look at Alexis, who is looking at him over the rim of her cup. He wants to believe everything she is saying, but it just sounds so far-fetched. How can he at least make her see that he hears her, even though belief in what she is saying is difficult at the moment?

"Aliens..." he says, eventually, not able to contain the uppermost question on his mind.

"Yes Tucker, extra-terrestrials!" She is emphatic and believable. But so is a good Hollywood actress.

"But how, and where? Surely we would have seen them. Aren't they slimy beings with large oval eyes?" Tucker has clearly seen too many movies.

"It's not like in the movies, Tucker. I mean think about

it, if human life could evolve on earth, ten fingers, ten toes, then what stopped it from happening elsewhere? Nothing! Under the right conditions, life can spring up anywhere. And I'm afraid that it's far more intelligent than we would like to believe." She is begging him to believe her now, knowing that if she had to tell this story one more time, she probably wouldn't even believe it.

"So intelligent life from other planets came to earth?" He has to repeat the statement in the form of a question just to make sure that he is hearing her right.

"Yes, Tucker..." Alexis is getting a little irritated with him since it is clear now that he doesn't believe her, probably just humoring her for the sake of.

She opens her laptop again and goes to pictures of the various weapons. When asked what he sees, Tucker says tools, farming implements. Then she goes to another picture with the spearhead flared so that all eight ends are visible. "Now what do you see?" she asks him.

"A weapon of some kind. So?" He really is confused, and Alexis doesn't hold this against him. This is after all her world, and these are her toys. She could possibly expect a New York City detective to get it.

"So, Tucker, this was found at a site that dated back to the Bronze Age. And this tool, this weapon, is titanium. Do you see where I'm going with this?"

He does see, but it's a very uncomfortable road for him to be on. Tucker just nods in agreement and then takes refuge in his cup. He wishes she had poured more whisky in it.

Tucker takes a deep breath and lets the information settle. He offers up his cup for a refill, sure to tell her not to go easy on the whisky. She doesn't know if he's joking or not, but just to be safe, she pours two extra shots of whisky in the cup this time. Hers remains the same single shot, however, not wanting to lose herself to the alcohol.

She hands him the cup, and as he takes it she looks him square in the face, deep into his brown eyes, and asks, "You do believe me, don't you?"

"Of course, I believe you. The question is just now, what are we going to do about it?" He really is at a bit of a loss, not quite believing her, so he needs her to lead the way.

"Well, I could stop my research for a while, just until this thing blows over." She tries to sound confident like she knows what she is talking about. But there is nothing to 'blow over', and when she picks up her research again, who knows what might happen?

"Is that even an option for you?" Tucker sees how passionate she is about what she does, and he knows that this is not even a possibility.

She searches her head for an answer while walking over to her ringing cell phone. Alexis looks at the screen, recognizing the prefix to the numbers but not registering it immediately. It's the World Government headquarters. "I'm sorry, I have to take this. It's work," she says, relieved at the reprieve she's been given by the phone call. She goes to take the call in the kitchen.

. . .

When she returns she is pale, as though she has just been told that someone had died.

"What is it Alexis," Tucker asks.

"It's the lab. There's been an explosion. I have to go!" She says this with an expressionless face, the blood taking forever to reach her cheeks. But then she is flushed, and she needs to sit down. Tucker comes in to hold her, to comfort her, not quite understanding her loss.

"It's okay," is all he can manage.

After a minute Alexis comes to her senses. There are things that need to be done. She needs to get down to the lab to see if anything can be saved. But it doesn't sound promising; the security guard who called her said that the place was completely gutted.

And it is. By the time Tucker and Alexis arrive the fire department has dowsed the flames. The elevator no longer goes to the basement. Alexis and Tucker, after much deliberation at the various checkpoints, have to take the emergency stairs. Even the stairwell is filled with smoke.

Alexis walks through the rubble, two floors, completely destroyed. Her office, and the lab. She walks in between desks and debris, wondering how, or what could have caused this explosion. And why were only the two floors damaged? She goes back to the stairwell and sees that there is another door, one floor down. But her finger wouldn't have gotten her to this level, and so she assumes that the door will be locked. Strangely enough, there doesn't seem to be any damage to this door.

"The fire department arrived just in time before the fire

could spread." A security guard tries to offer her an explanation. But it still doesn't explain why the explosions were so contained.

She gets a list of all the people that worked on the two floors that are no more, with their numbers. She must tell them what has happened. She wonders if she shouldn't perhaps get Grant's take on the situation first before she goes and gives people the day off, or days off, depending on how long it will be before they manage to get the repairs done. She wonders if Grant even knows about the explosion. But how can he not, he was probably the first person they called.

Alexis gets through the list, everyone getting the generic 'there's been an explosion; we'll let you know when to return to work'. She has to dial Chloe twice before she picks up, sounding out of breath, like she's been running, or having sex.

"Oh my god, that's terrible," is the response she gets, but since this is the general response she has gotten from everybody, it doesn't bother her much.

"So yeah, I'll call you." Alexis dismisses her and hangs up the phone, not really caring that Chloe's brother is standing right behind her.

"Is that everyone?" Tucker asks, looking over her shoulder at the list.

"Yes, I think so."

"Let's get out of here, there's nothing more you can do here anyway." Tucker is too practical, given that Alexis has just lost a large chunk of her life. But she has to concede that there really is nothing that she can do except wait for the World Government to get in touch regarding the repairs. So they leave.

He takes her to a place across town that is famed for its tikka chicken. "I hope you like spicy food," he says, as he parks the car.

"I can handle it," Alexis responds, still a little distracted by what has just happened and what she has just seen.

"That's not what I asked..." Tucker really cares enough to make sure that she isn't just doing anything for the sake of, and that she really wants to be doing it. "Do you like spicy food?" He rephrases the question for her benefit.

"Yes I do," Alexis replies, trying to sound as convincing as possible. She really is neither here nor there on the issue of spicy food.

"Good!" Tucker says, knowing that it is going to be difficult to distract her from what's on her mind. He makes a decent go of it though, and before long they are laughing over grilled chicken quarters lathered in tikka sauce. Even Alexis has to admit that it's actually very, very good.

By the time Tucker gets her home, she has all but forgotten the events of the afternoon. She will deal with them tomorrow. For now, she just wants to bathe and get to bed. She says goodnight to Tucker in the foyer, despite his eyes saying that he would like nothing more than to be let up again. But Alexis is not that kind of girl. And she actually likes him, so she has to play it cool.

. . .

She is woken the next day by a driver. His call comes in just after 7 AM. And it takes her a minute to figure out that she doesn't recognize the voice on the other end of the line. He has been sent by Grant Chambers to pick her up, he would like to see her.

Alexis gets into the shower, her mind racing. What could the president of the world want from her, when all he had to do was call her to let her know about the lab? She wonders how she should dress, and decides to dress as she would if she were going to the office. But this is anything but a normal day at the office. The office doesn't exist anymore, and never, not once, has a car ever been sent for her. She takes longer than is necessary to get ready, trying to buy herself time to figure things out.

"Hello my dear, come through," Grant says, as Alexis steps into the freezing office. She can't wait for him to offer her a drink. "It's a pity about the lab, all that work. But take the time to regroup, and I'm sure you will be able to pick up where you left off." He speaks while pouring the drink that he hasn't even asked her if she wants. She practically grabs it out of his hands.

"Yes, a pity," she says, shivering through her first few sips of the alcohol that will warm her despite it really being too early for her to be drinking. She watches Grant in his shorts, moving around the office as casually as though it was a summer's day. He must really suffer from a thermo-regulation problem, because nothing else explains how he can cope with the temperature in the office, with nothing but shorts and a t-shirt on.

"So we'll get this mess sorted out, and then everyone can come back to work. At least you still have the bunkers to keep you busy." She doesn't know if this is an order to keep working, or if he genuinely feels for her and what she has lost, but she dismisses this as she takes another drink from him, feeling the cold even through her large coat and jeans. It really is as cold as a freezer up here.

"Yes, at least there's that." She references the bunkers as though they could never be as important as the work she had been doing at the lab, and all her files in her office. Grant just laughs, a dry giggle really, as he motions for them to sit. She does as she is told, wanting to fish and see whether he knows more about the explosions that he is saying.

"Come now my dear, it could have been a lot worse. There might have been lives lost if this explosion happened on any other day. Perhaps even yours. And that would have been a great loss to the world of archeology, I would imagine."

"Yes, you're right. This explosion was timed perfectly," she says, looking for even the semblance of emotion from him. He gives up nothing if indeed he knows anything. Grant just gets up, pours her a third drink, and comes to sit right next to her, putting a hand on her shoulder. She isn't sure if she is supposed to find this comforting, but what it is, is very cold. Even through her coat, she can feel that he is very cold indeed, probably just a side effect from being in this freezer all day.

She sits and sips the third drink in silence, enjoying the maturity of the scotch. Grant just watches her, catching her eyes every time she looks up, both of them forcing a smile. She really just wants to be out of here now, and with three of the expensive scotches in her, she has the guts to excuse herself. But not before she asks him what particular brand of whisky it is that she has been drinking. She leaves the penthouse with a sealed bottle of her own.

Alexis cracks open the bottle as soon as she gets home. It's not even noon yet, but she feels like she needs it. Actually, she wants it, more for its taste than its effect. She pours herself a drink, and just breaths in the aroma, mimicking Grant. She can almost understand why he enjoys the smell of the scotch. It's rich and woody, earthy textures playing with her senses.

She takes out her laptop and opens it. She lets the screen open up and then she navigates to the slides. She can't resist sipping the scotch any longer, and takes a huge swig, pressing the button that will turn it into a slideshow.

She watches the slides as they appear, one in front of the other, and as the scotch settles inside her, she lets the pictures move through her head. The screen fades in and out, the pictures merging to form one continuous stream.

It feels like a dream, she isn't sure if it's the impact of the scotch, or maybe the nagging pressure of her not knowing what will become of her, from her opening up her laptop. She looks around, almost as though she expects to find a camera or two, carefully hidden in the corners of her ceiling. But she sees nothing.

By the time she's on her second scotch, she starts to get a little more paranoid, and she gets up and starts to turn the whole apartment inside out, looking for something, anything that resembles a bug. She finds nothing. It would be very difficult for someone to hide anything in her minimalist apartment.

She goes back to her slides and opens her notebook on the side. Feeling safer now that she has checked her apartment, and now that she is away from the prying eyes of the World Government, she recommits herself to her work.

Before long she has so many notes open on the bed that she has to move to her desk. She plugs in her laptop and continues to reference the slides with the notes, coming to the same dead ends she did when she worked back in her old office. But she persists, and eventually, it pays off.

She goes with her hunch, that the numbers on the calendars are numbers of people or beings, and not years, and suddenly it all starts to fall into place. She realizes that the number of aliens sent has been relative to the world's population and that these extra-terrestrials must have come before the natural disaster happened. They must have kept pockets of humanity alive, how; she still has to figure out and then placed these pockets of humanity back on earth, to start the whole planet up again. But for what?

Why would aliens want to keep the human race going, when we're doing such a stellar job of destroying ourselves? This is the million-dollar question; one that she will get to after dinner. She thinks of calling Tucker to let her know what progress she has made. Actually, she thinks of calling him just for the sake of. But it's a weeknight, and he's probably working. So she goes out to eat alone, feeling exhilarated and nervous all at the same time, but the scotch has definitely done a good job of taking the edge off.

Alexis is losing count of the number of times she has eaten out in the last two weeks. It's certainly one time too many, and she makes a mental note that this needs to change. She makes a lot of mental notes and feels that she might just get to some of them now that she doesn't have an office to report to.

She gets back to find the chaos disturbed. She remembers locking the door before she left, she double-checked. But here, in her bedroom, is a man, probably the same man with the fingers that smelt like tobacco, going through her things. It's too late for her to try to get to the front door, and screaming for help would be like screaming into a tin, nobody would hear her. Each apartment is designed in such a way that you never had to hear your neighbors, or see them for that matter.

"What do you want?" She steels herself against the man now coming towards her, looking as if he might punch her. Instead, he moves quickly behind her and closes the bedroom door, locking it so that it's just Alexis and this strange man with smelly fingers in her bedroom.

"Sit down!" he barks, and she obeys. He proceeds to go through her work as though he knows what he is looking for, but clearly, he doesn't, judging by the pieces of paper he lets fall to the floor. He presses the arrow key on her laptop so that the pictures move more swiftly by, passing ones that she would have lingered on so that she knows he is just hired muscle.

"What do you want" she repeats, trying to sound more threatening than she is.

"I warned you to stop with this, didn't I?" He looks at her as he says this, and Alexis can make out a burn on his face, or a birthmark, she isn't sure. The only light in the room comes from the bedside lamp on the opposite side of the bed.

"Who are you, and what has any of this to do with you anyways?" She doesn't expect him to answer, doesn't want him to, in case she doesn't like the answer she gets. But it only seems right that she knows what the hell is going on in her own apartment, and why this stranger feels like he can go through her stuff.

"You don't want to know who I am," he snarls, and she gets the picture. She watches as he goes through her work, not really looking for anything in particular, just making chaos of the chaos.

When he is done destroying her computer and ripping her notes apart, he leaves without a further word. Alexis wants to know who he is, and who sent him, but these are answers she is obviously not going to get. She even follows him into the hallway and out the front door, screaming behind him for him to answer her. But cool as a cucumber, he just exits her apartment and heads past the elevators to the stairwell. She lets it go.

But this time she calls Tucker immediately, and he arrives in ten minutes. He'd actually been circling her block, trying to process what all she had said to him. Still not convinced, the mess in her apartment lets him know that aliens or no aliens, Alexis is in danger. He has no choice now but to help her.

The question is just, how?

. . .

He pours them both a drink from the bottle she received from Grant, thick shots, no ice, both of them needing the drink for exactly the same reason now. He puts a hand on her back and lets it move up and down her tiny back until the alcohol takes effect. She just sighs a loud relieved sigh, now that Tucker is here.

"Have you touched anything?" he asks her, looking at the mess surrounding her desk.

"No, but I don't want to call the police, not yet. What would I say to them? Besides, he just came back to warn me to stop what I'm doing again, no harm done." She tries to reassure him of things that she herself is so longer sure of.

"No harm done, what do you mean? Some guy breaks into your apartment and..."

"No Tucker, no cops. Not yet! Well, maybe just one..." She looks up at him and smiles, seeing in his eyes that he believes her now, and knowing that he will help her.

CHAPTER 7

ALEXIS DECIDES to show Tucker the bunkers. When they arrive, the security guards on duty give Tucker a weird look, not sure what to make of him, and not sure whether or not they should let him through. He produces his badge, which seems to placate the guards somewhat, but the looks go nowhere.

She opens the first bunker, and Tucker walks through the rows and rows of boxes, not sure what he is looking at, and definitely not sure if he can open them up. He looks at Alexis for confirmation, and she nods 'go ahead'. He does.

By the time they get to the third bunker, Tucker is exhausted. Something about being surrounded by all this stuff that he can't make sense of exhausts him. But he persists, for Alexis's sake, appreciating that she has let him into her world like this. It's definitely a step in the right direction.

When they arrive at the seventh bunker the key won't fit. Alexis has used this key before, and she has marked it so that she knows it's the right key. Still, she tries all the others. None of them fit.

· · ·

She looks at Tucker, hoping for a suggestion. But Tucker is exhausted from the previous six bunkers, and it's getting quite late. Still, Alexis looks at him, hoping that he will read her mind and use some muscle to get them into the bunker. If someone went through the effort to change the locks on this particular bunker, there must be a good reason. And it's this reason that Alexis wants to find out.

Tucker looks around for something to pry open the lock. There's nothing. He looks over to the guardhouse and knows that they will hear a gunshot. But he has no choice, so he pulls out his service weapon. You would think that a thousand years would have been long enough for them to come up with a weapon that didn't make so much noise when it was fired. No such luck.

"Stand back," he cautions Alexis, who is already standing behind him, her hands over her ears.

He fires straight at the lock, a single shot that brings the guards running, their own batons in hand. Thank goodness these amateurs don't carry real weapons, or else the pair might have been in some real trouble.

"Hey, you can't do that," yells one of the guards, careful as he approaches the man with the loaded gun. Tucker lifts his badge, showing them that he can. Reluctantly the guards return the batons to their holsters, but they both look at the door with the lock now dangling, also curious as to what might be inside.

Tucker removes the dangling lock and opens the door. He fumbles for the light switch so that Alexis is the first to find it. She flicks it up, and the room is soaked once more in the same clinical white light as the other six. Their eyes take a minute to adjust, this room a little messier than the others. It's as if the contents were brought here in a hurry, and they hadn't had the time yet to box everything. Actually, there is no sign of boxes, the rows of neatly lined crates conspicuously absent.

Alexis looks at the items, and she recognizes them immediately. They're from the destroyed lab. All the debris has been collected here, like a scrapyard. She lovingly attends to each piece, holding each one with the solemn affection that one would show a dead child.

The room is a deathly silence. Nobody dares speak, seeing the attention that Alexis is giving them, almost understanding her loss now. Tucker wants to reach out and touch her, hold her and tell her that everything is going to be fine. But he thinks better of it and just hangs back and watches her work.

"The damage to these is minimal," she says, stating the obvious.

"You're right," Tucker agrees, although he had no idea of what the items looked like before.

"No, I'm serious Tucker. Except for smoke damage, much of which can just be wiped away with a cloth, these artifacts are intact. It's remarkable."

Tucker really has no response for her, just accepting that very few things have been completely destroyed. The only things that seem to have been obliterated are the artifacts that actually were from the period they had been placed in. These other-worldly artifacts, these weapons, are all relatively intact.

The guards have no idea what they are looking at, and one of them reaches for an artifact. He is quickly reprimanded so that they both know not to touch anything. After a minute they decide to leave Alexis to it, Tucker too, and they return to their station, unsure of whether they should let their superiors know that the senior archeologist rocked up at the bunkers with a gun-wielding cop who just blew the lock on bunker number seven to smithereens. They decide to give it a moment, probably fearful of what the trigger-happy Tucker might do to them if they should report this prematurely.

Inside the bunker, Alexis is done tending to her dead children. She moves a few of them out of the way to make for seating on one of the shelves. But it's an uncomfortable seat, her back bent by the upper shelf. She needs to sit down though, just to take a moment to process everything that is happening.

And it is still happening. She feels like there are forces at play all around her, forces that she has no control over, working hard to stop her from the discovery she's already made. And these forces, it seems, are coming from the World Government. But why?

Why would they be so against her work here, and why would they keep these artifacts locked up here, in bunker seven, and not tell her? These questions start to work on her until she just needs to leave the bunker. She gets up, taking a moment to straighten up after the shelf has done some serious work on her back.

But just one more thing to check, she goes through the rows of artifacts, looking for something that clearly isn't here. There are no hard drives from the many computers that were in her lab, and certainly none from her office. Maybe they stored these elsewhere. Or maybe they were completely destroyed in the explosion and rendered uselessly. There are also none of her files in the bunker. She had been told that the filing cabinet was fire-resistant; clearly, it was not explosive proof. Or maybe, just maybe, these too are being kept elsewhere to be perused by whoever was responsible for the explosion.

She suddenly feels like she needs to see Grant Chambers. But how, now that her finger will probably not even get her in the building until the repairs to the lab are done? They leave the bunker, with the lock replaced to its original position, but not serving any real purpose.

They need to get into the World Government headquarters, too many unanswered questions floating around in Alexis's head. She needs to see Grant Chambers, and she needs to see just how much effort they are putting into getting the lab and her offices sorted out.

But it's late now, really late, and they haven't eaten. They haven't even thought of food, even though their stomachs have been begging for something, anything, for the longest time now. But Alexis has no energy for a restaurant. Even smiling courteously at a waiter would be too much for her to handle right now.

"Take out, my place?" Tucker suggests.

"Yeah sure, whatever's fine," she responds without thinking. And before she can raise any sort of objection they arrive at Tucker's front gate just as the Chinese delivery guy pulls up. He made the call on their way, sensing correctly that Alexis just needs to be away from all these questions.

They go upstairs, to the same lounging area where Alexis looked so comfortable, and eat out of the boxes, with no time for plates and no need for the formality. Tucker opens a bottle of red, hoping that Alexis will wind down somewhat now, even if she just sleeps.

"Don't you have to work tomorrow?" she asks him, as he pours their second glass of wine.

"I will be, with you. This is a case now, although not officially. If anybody asks me about it I'll just say that I'm following up on some leads. The paperwork can wait." He reassures her that he is there for her until she has the answers she so desperately seeks, or at least until she has no more questions.

And Alexis needs this reassurance. She is starting to feel like the walls are closing in on her so that it even becomes difficult to breathe. She looks out over the view of the suburb, all the lights, each one a part of a home or the street, and she wishes that she was asleep in one of those bedrooms right now and that she had a normal job to go to in the morning.

. . .

But this is not the case. She is caught in the middle of something that is definitely bigger than she is. Much bigger! She catches Tucker looking at her and she realizes she must be a mess. Why hadn't she insisted that he drop her at her house? Now she is here, in his space, a very big space, but she is unable to escape his gaze.

He is careful now about his next move, knowing that he needs to be there for Alexis, and so not wanting to compromise his ability to do that with a one-night stand. After all, she hasn't alluded to them being anything more than friends, and it's definitely too soon for them to jump into bed together. But the thought keeps surfacing so that Tucker has to look away from Alexis to try and shake the thought from him.

But then Alexis is standing behind him, her arms reaching around him, her head resting on his broad back. She has left her drink on the side table, but Tucker still has his, and he takes a huge sip from it, emptying the glass. He wants to turn around, but he can't, his body already giving away what is going on in his head.

She comes around him, thankfully not looking down, her eyes on his. She takes his face in her hands, practically having to stand on her toes because Tucker is so tall. She closes her eyes and waits, waits for him to come to her. She has met him halfway, and now it would be up to him. He can't hide his excitement, rubbing it against her now as he goes down to kiss her. She smiles into the kiss, feeling what might have been embarrassing if they weren't two consenting adults.

They kiss for a long time, enjoying the taste of each other. It will probably not go any further than kissing tonight, but one thing is sure, they are definitely sexually attracted to one another.

. . .

They wake up in each other's arms, fully clothed so that they know that nothing happened. Although both of them wanted something to happen, desperately, they respect one another enough to know to tread carefully. Alexis makes breakfast while Tucker showers, and then he finishes up while she cleans up. They eat comfortably, neither of them feeling awkward about all that kissing.

After a quick stop at Alexis's apartment so that she can get changed, they head for the World Government. Alexis hopes that the elevator is still down and that the only way to the basement is the staircase. No fancy retinal scan is required to get onto the staircase, and she needs to get back down there.

After confirming that her finger and eye will not get her into the building anymore, they resort to Tucker's trusty badge. It gets them through every single security checkpoint on the outside of the building, and once inside, it gets them passed the three checkpoints that lead to the elevator. Right next to the lift is the entrance to the staircase, a fire escape so that it is not guarded as heavily as the elevators, just one security guard who seems to have other things on his mind so he just waves them through when they say they are just going to check out the lab.

But it's not the burnt-out lab that Alexis is interested in. She wants to try and get into the two stories underneath what used to be her lab and office. The question is how? How is Alexis going to get into the real basement of the building without stirring up too much attention?

· · ·

Cameras are mounted strategically above each of the staircases. So she is not going to be able to pry the door open without being seen. And Tucker won't be able to use his gun either, the building too quiet for this to go by unnoticed. But there just must be a way to get into that room. Whatever it is, neither Tucker nor Alexis knows what it is.

They step off the small landing into the old lab. There has clearly not even been a cleanup team dispatched here yet. They just collected all the artifacts and took them to bunker number seven. Other than that, nothing has happened here.

Walking amongst the debris of tabletops and surfaces, chairs and glass, Alexis tries to piece together what happened here. But she is not an explosives expert so that all she knows is that the place blew up.

Tucker can actually understand what Alexis is feeling now. If somebody blew up the station and he was not able to go to work, he would be devastated. Clearly, she loved her job as much as he loves his.

Alexis keeps expecting them to be interrupted, by guards, or even Grant Chambers. She finds it strange that she cannot get into the building without the assistance of a police officer, but now, once inside, she is left to roam freely. Well, not that freely. As long as she stays in the lab, or dares to go to the office, or rather what's left of it, she will be fine. Cameras are closely watching the two move through the old lab, not touching anything, but questioning everything.

Uppermost on Alexis's mind though is the room underneath them. She has no idea what is inside it, she never even knew of its existence until they used the stairs for the first time when her lab exploded. It might even just be parking, but she doesn't think so. Something pulls her towards it so that she knows that there is much more to the locked doors than meets the eye.

Then there is a commotion in the hallway, and Tucker and Alexis hide in the old lab as best they can. But they still have a clear view of the staircase. They are both not sure if the commotion is after them, but there is no time to think about this. Alexis must be breathing too loud because Tucker places his hand over her mouth. His free hand releases his gun from its holster.

The staircase fills with men that Alexis doesn't recognize. But then someone comes into view that both she and Tucker know. Chloe moves to the front, between all the men, and uses her access card to get them into the lower level. They both can't believe what they are seeing, and Tucker removes his hand from Alexis's mouth so that she can turn and look at him. Both of them mouth 'Chloe', before they go in for a closer look.

But the door closes behind the last of the men to go inside, and Alexis knows from experience that it is probably locked. They are both flabbergasted, and for a second they walk toward the elevator before realizing that it no longer works. They need to get out of here, and fast before the guard upstairs remembers them and tells Chloe that they're in the building.

. . .

The pair gets back to the staircase, and they watch the door at the bottom of it for a while. When it's clear that nobody is coming out, they rush to the top of the staircase, and after gathering themselves, they exit through the door that is slightly ajar. To their relief, the security guard is busy chatting to his colleagues so that they just slip past him.

Tucker raises his badge and they are let through the security checkpoints that will get them out of the building. Once outside, Alexis exhales hard, not sure what to make of what she has just seen. It's late, too late for Chloe to be working on anything even vaguely related to archeology, so what was she doing there?

"Chloe?" Alexis asks eventually.

"Yeah, let's get out of here. This place gives me the creeps." Tucker shows Alexis the goose flesh on his arm that has nothing to do with the weather, and so using his badge, he gets them off the property of the World Government. Soon they are in a cozy little pub on the arty side of town, needing to disappear into the strangeness of New York City for a while, and needing a drink.

"Do you think she knows we were there?" Alexis asks Tucker as their drinks arrive.

"No, if she did, we would have known about it. Any idea what she was doing there?" Tucker needs to get an understanding of what Alexis's job actually is, and what part Chloe plays in everything so that he knows whether or not to be suspicious of what he's just seen.

"Not a clue, and she seemed to be in charge, didn't she?" Alexis asks for confirmation of what she saw, needing to hear it from somebody else so that she knew for sure that her job was no longer safe.

"Yeah, she did. But I thought you were her boss?" Tucker has to ask.

"So did I!" Alexis lets him know that she really has no clue of what is going on here, and she then raises her glass, signaling a waiter that it needs to be refilled.

Tucker knows better than to pursue any line of questioning that will make things any more awkward for Alexis. She really looks lost suddenly, as if someone stole her ice cream. He wants to hold her, but he knows that she just needs to process what's just happened. Perhaps they're seeing things, perhaps they're just chasing ghosts, but something is definitely going on in that room, and they need to find out what.

But the security is way too impenetrable. They got lucky tonight, Alexis knows this. And they probably won't be so lucky again. The guards at the World Government really seemed a little complacent tonight, but she doesn't expect them to be as complacent the next time around. And there has to be a next time.

Over burgers they discuss the room, and what it possibly contains. They can't think of anything that could possibly be on the other side of that door that requires so much secrecy, having Chloe come in the middle of the night, accompanied by men who look like they come fresh from a ship of refugees give or take one or two guards. It all just seems really unnecessary. Unless there was something in that room that needed the manpower, perhaps other artifacts, larger ones. But then why would Chloe have been called in to receive it and not her? They trusted her with the bunkers, so why not with this room?

. . .

"Unless I've got this all wrong, and they really are just doing research work down there, something that doesn't concern me." Even saying it sounds absurd. Everything concerns her that has anything to do with her staff. Unless Chloe was no longer a member of her staff. "I need to see Grant Chambers," she says, in between bites.

"Who, the president?" Tucker asks, not knowing that it was even possible to just request a meeting with the man.

"Yip, he will have the answers that I need. Nothing happens in that building without him knowing about it. And if I've been fired, he can at least say it to my face." She tries to sound like she doesn't care. But the truth is, she does care. This job was the best thing that ever happened to her. She was going places.

"Are you sure you wanna do that?" Tucker's concern is genuine. There is something going on at the World Government that he isn't sure of yet. And he needs to be sure before Alexis goes talking to the president. If nothing happened there without his knowledge, then he must know about that room, and he must know why Chloe is in charge of whatever it is that's going on there. His gut tells him that talking to the president right now would be counterproductive.

"I'm not sure about anything right now Tucker," Alexis is at her wit's end. Everything she thought she understood about life has been turned on its head, and now there's this secret room with its midnight visitors. She has to get into that room, and the key to getting in there is sitting across the table from her. "You could clone Chloe's access cards," she says after a long time, obviously wanting it to run through her head a few times before it came out of her mouth.

He looks at her for a while, thinking about what she's just asked him. Actually, he's thinking about how he can make it possible, without his astute sister knowing. Being a detective doesn't mean you're a good spy, far from it. And Tucker definitely isn't a good spy.

He wants to ask her 'how', but he knows that she is trusting that he will know-how. She trusts him for a lot of things lately, with a lot of things. He likes it. They're getting close, and it's very obvious. But they both tread that fine line between respecting one another, and plain down fear. They're scared of one another, for their own reasons, scared to go over that line between making out, and being in a relationship. Making out is less complicated. They've both seen their fair share of complicated relationships in the past.

Well actually, one each. But it was complicated enough to still have them scared and torn.

They move the conversation on to other things, Alexis certain that she's been heard, and that her request will be met. They talk easily with each other, and by the time they check it's 3 AM, and they're both not even tired. But common sense dictates that Alexis needs to sleep in her own bed, and this is exactly what she does after Tucker has dropped her off.

. . .

By the time Tucker meets his sister the following week for their usual date he's as ready as he's going to be. He just has to hope that she has her access cards in her purse since she's still technically 'on leave'. He stands up as she arrives, and she sits without him kissing her for the first time since they started this ritual.

She doesn't even notice, her mind obviously preoccupied with the task she has been given by the World Government. Chloe waits just long enough for her first drink to arrive, then she excuses herself, needing the bathroom, as usual. Tucker has come to expect this dance from her, knowing that even if she pitches for their dinners, she would rather be doing something else.

Chloe clearly has no reason to think that her brother would find anything interesting in her purse, because she takes her phone and her compact out of it, and then leaves it hanging on the back of her chair. Tucker takes the only gap he knows he will have during this dinner to get into her purse.

As soon as Chloe disappears around a corner he places his hand in her bag and feels around. Her bag isn't as put together as she is, and he fumbles through a million miscellaneous items before his fingers run over what feels like what he is looking for. He lifts the cards out of the bag carefully, like they might break if he were handling them any rougher than he needs to.

He takes a cloning machine out of his jacket pocket and starts to run each one through the slot. He is nervous, almost too nervous for a seasoned police officer. But he keeps reminding himself that he can do this, that he is a detective with the New York City police, and that he can definitely clone a few cards.

By the time she returns he is done, the cards back in the mixed bag of goodies that he cares very little for. She sits, ready to order, and to hurry things along so that she can get out of here. Tucker has to restrain himself from asking her about the room, at least until he and Alexis have managed to get a look inside.

"So, how's Alexis," Chloe starts.

"She's doing as well as can be expected, given that she doesn't have anything to do at the moment." Tucker bites his tongue, fighting back the urge to just ask her what's really on his mind.

"Surely she's enjoying the break," Chloe fishes, wanting to know where Alexis's head is at, not wanting the details of her 'enjoyment'.

"To be honest I think she's really struggling. She really loved her job," Tucker is getting closer to just blurting it out.

"She still has a job, just nowhere to do it, yet." Chloe sounds so sure of herself that Tucker can't help but think that she knows more than she is letting on.

"You're right. I'm sure. But still, it's hard for her you know." Tucker needs to test if his sister has any sympathy for Alexis.

"Of course I'm right. So, are we going to order?" Chloe moves the conversation along before her brother gives up any details of the time he's been spending with her arch-nemesis.

. . .

Once dinner is over Tucker goes straight for Alexis's apartment, not wanting to wait for another second, needing to get to the bottom of this. He waits for her downstairs, in the foyer. As soon as she appears out of the elevator he takes her by the arm and leads her to where his car is parked.

Inside the car he takes out the cloning machine, and takes out a few dummy cards, giving her instructions on how to clone them as he drives in the direction of the World Government. By the time they arrive, she has managed to clone every single one of Chloe's cards.

It takes a little more time to get through the checkpoints on the outside of the building, the guards probably buying time while they let Grant Chambers know that Alexis is here, again. He doesn't seem to object to this, because soon enough they're inside the building. They head straight for the staircase, and after a brief consultation with the security guard parked at the entrance, they're inside the old lab again.

It looks like some work has been done here now, in terms of cleaning it up at least. Now the space is just a large expanse, Alexis not noticing before just how big this place was. But thinking about it now, it runs the length of the building, so it makes sense. Seeing it all cleaned up, even in the dark, it looks sterile, more so than it was when it was her lab and she tinkered around with her toys in it.

"Shall we?" Tucker can see that Alexis is stalling, probably not wanting the confirmation of whatever is going on in the floor underneath them.

"Yes, let's do this," she sounds surer than she is, and she hands the cards to Tucker, following him out of the old lab, onto the landing, and then down the stairs. She is suddenly a ball of nerves.

The third card gets them into the 'lab'. The door hisses for a second, and then the sound of a very complicated mechanism sounds too loud in the darkened silence. They both step back and wait. The door hisses again, and then it seems to lift off of its hinges. It opens outwards, towards them, so that they have to step even further back on the landing.

They look at each other, then at the door. This is what they wanted, and if there is indeed someone behind the camera mounted in the corner of the stairwell, they won't be alone for very long. But Alexis is hesitant about going inside the open door now, knowing that the answers to all her questions lie just beyond it.

"It's now or never," Tucker muses, almost under his breath, anticipating a barrage of security men to storm the staircase at any time. Alexis is silent, trying to control her breathing, unsure what it is that has her so spooked. It's just a door, an open one, and on the other side could be the answers to a whole lot of her questions. She steels herself and takes a hold of Tucker's jacket from behind.

Tucker steps into the space cautiously; his firearm locked and loaded. But they hadn't seen anybody coming into the room, so they know they should be alone on the other side of the huge steel door. Alexis wonders how the explosion rattled the door to the lab but left this one pretty much intact. She wonders a lot of things as she and Tucker make steady but cautious progress into the room.

They search for a light switch, although this is not necessary. They give up the search, making their way to the first row of the coffin-like chambers, a green glow coming from inside so that any additional light is really unnecessary. What the hell?!

The door hisses, and shuts with a thud, so that they both look away from the chambers for a moment, in the direction of the door. But Alexis knows how the doors work at the World Government by now. And she is certain that they will be able to get out when they need to.

She looks on with amazement, and Tucker is completely dumbfounded. They both just stare into the glass coffins, their jaws on the ground.

CHAPTER 8

ALEXIS STARES IN AMAZEMENT, as does Tucker. They cannot believe what they are looking at. Rows and rows of chambers, each one containing an extra-terrestrial, and each alien still alive, line the large room. What is this place? And how long has it been here? Alexis's questions now have questions.

They move silently between the rows of extra-terrestrials, seemingly trapped inside these glass coffins. Tubes come out of the sides of these and lead into large tanks, probably gas, whatever it is that these aliens breathe on their native planets. It is a truly remarkable sight.

Some of them really look like aliens. Visions from science-fiction films, right there in front of them, so close that they could simply reach out and touch them if it wasn't for the glass. Tendrils and tentacles protrude from the necks of some, the heads of others; so that you would think that you were in a museum dedicated to what life on other planets might look like if it existed.

Others look remarkably ordinary, human even, except for the pipes sticking out of them. What the hell was going on here, what was this? Alexis finds that the more questions she asks, the more she has. So she decides that just for the moment, she will enjoy the sheer spectacle of it all. Who would have thought, that in her lifetime, she would be witness to such a marvel? Certainly not her!

It would take them the remainder of the night to go through each and every chamber, so they don't even try. But something about the aliens she has seen so far reminds Alexis of something else. She searches her head but comes up short, still not fully comprehending that she is standing in the midst of live aliens. What is it about these beings though that feels like déjà vu?

Then it hits her. She has seen them before. Each and every one of these aliens have come across her desk, in the form of an idol, or a sketch from a time forgotten. She recognizes them as the gods of many ancient peoples, gods that she thought were just the imaginings of a people with too much time on their hands. But now she knows better. Now she realizes that each of these beings, probably several of them at a time, have visited ancient tribes. And what we thought were imaginary gods created for the purpose of controlling the population, were actual alien beings who walked on earth.

How is it then that we have managed to capture these beings, so revered by our ancestors? And why, what purpose does it serve to house them here, all in one place, keeping them alive? What questions do we want them to answer? She can think of a million questions that she would like to ask just one of the aliens, anyone, and has to fight back the urge to tap on the glass in case she actually wakes one.

Alexis needs to sit, but there are no chairs in this 'lab'. There are no tables either. There are just these rows and rows of extra-terrestrials surrounding what feels like a court-yard the size of half a football field. All of them face towards this courtyard, which seems to have no real significance.

So Alexis had it all wrong. Human beings were actually the ones capturing aliens. But how could this be, with our prim-itive technology and backward ways? How is it that we managed to outsmart those who are obviously much smarter than we are? This is a question she knows will be best answered by Grant Chambers, but how, when he has no idea that she is in here, or that she knows about their alien stockpile?

Alexis takes a closer look at one of the chambers. There is a label underneath it, at the foot of the alien it contains. She reads it once, not really processing. She reads it again, and again. Things start to come into focus. She moves on to the next one, reading it more carefully. She reads five of these labels before it becomes clear to her.

She realizes what each label contains, the information on it methodical, all the same, yet different in detail. It's these details that interest her most. She reads a couple more, not speaking to Tucker now, going into archeological mode.

. . .

They are details of the beings, where they come from, and what it would take for them to survive the earth and its atmosphere. They all seem capable of surviving on earth outside of these chambers, but not for very long. So the chambers are designed to keep each one of them strong enough to survive on earth. But survive for what?

She wishes that she had brought her notebook, or any book for that matter so that she can make notes. But with no such equipment, she pulls out her cell phone and uses it to take pictures of the being, and of the label underneath it. Each time she takes a picture the flash goes off, reading the light in the room so that the flash is necessary. She is scared that the flash will wake one of these monsters, but nothing. They seem content to just lie inside these glass coffins, with no intention to stir any time soon.

Actually, they seem too content in these sarcophagi, and Alexis is certain that she sees a smile on some of the faces. Perhaps it's not a smile, she tries to assure herself. Perhaps it is just the way their faces seem to have contorted in the liquid that houses them. But still, it's uncanny.

She knows that she won't get to all of them, not today, and makes a note to return. Not a mental note mind you, she has enough of those swimming around inside her head. She turns to Tucker and speaks to him for the first time in what feels like forever.

"We need to come back here, soon." She looks at him as she says this, hoping that the urgency of this discovery registers with him too.

· · ·

"Yeah, sure, but it's really getting late now, and we probably need to get out of here, before someone comes looking for us." Tucker is speaking for his stomach, which is grumbling loudly. One thing about being a detective is that you always make time to eat, no matter what is going on. This habit takes him over completely when he is hungry. And now, he is very hungry.

Alexis realizes that Tucker probably wants to get out of here, the entire episode is too much for him and his one-sided brain activity. It takes a very creative individual to be as unfazed as she is around these extra-terrestrials. She almost expected that the research she was working on would lead them to something like this. Tucker not!

She looks at her watch, it's almost ten. They are lost in the maze of aliens until they get to the center of the room, to the courtyard-like space. Then they try to get their bearings, not sure suddenly which way is out.

Alexis sits on the floor, much to Tucker's surprise, and closes her eyes. She is thinking hard, trying to remember the first aliens they saw, which would give them an idea of which way to go. Tucker usually has such good navigating skills, but the extra-terrestrials around them have really messed with his head.

Alexis raises a hand which shuts Tucker up. She needs to think. She looks at her phone, remembering the pictures that she took. Looking at them from the beginning should give her an idea of which way they should go. She gives Tucker her hand and he helps her up. She thinks she knows which way to go now.

. . .

But they had underestimated just how far into the room they had come. And although they are walking in the right direction, it seems like they are walking forever. Tucker is well and truly confused, not even sure if they are going the right way. Alexis on the other hand is sure, but just how long it will take them to reach the door, she doesn't know. Hand in hand, they keep on moving.

"Are you sure that this is the right way," Tucker asks her eventually when every chamber starts to look like every other chamber.

"Yes, I'm sure. Just keep on moving." Alexis assures him that they are definitely moving in the right direction.

The glow becomes a deep orange, and the two stop and stare for a while at one chamber in particular. It seems to be pumping more gas into the chamber, the liquid draining from it. They notice the next chamber also draining the liquid, more gas being pumped into the chamber. Again they stop, looking at the chambers that seem to be coming to life, and the nerves surface quickly.

"What's going on?" Tucker whispers.

"I don't know!" Alexis whispers back, loudly. "But we need to get out of here as soon as possible." She is pulling Tucker along now, Tucker looking in awe at the chambers that are now emptying.

"Wait, Alexis, wait," Tucker really wants to see what will happen now, his gun ready to fire. He thinks that his gun will stand between them and the aliens that seem to be coming to life.

"No Tucker, let's go, now," Alexis really just wants to get out of here now, and get away from these aliens. Maybe this is just a shift that happens periodically, perhaps that changing of the liquid is essential to keeping these aliens alive, but Alexis doesn't care. She is really scared now, and this is something that she had not expected. Tucker was the one who was nervous, more nervous than she had been. But now, the shoe is definitely on the other foot.

They move to the back of the rows now, towards the wall. This is because the chambers towards the back of the room are not active, yet. They get to the wall, and move against it, in the crawlspaces behind the chambers that line the wall, towards the exit. Alexis checks her phone to make sure that they're still moving in the right direction.

Tucker and Alexis can only imagine how many other such labs are in existence. They wonder again without saying what's the purpose of these labs might be. But it doesn't feel like a lab. It feels like a gathering place for extra-terrestrials, and if it wasn't for the fact that each of these beings was in a chamber, seemingly isolated from the outside world, it would look like they were having a mass meeting.

Alexis's head suddenly fills with everything that she's discovered over the last while. She wonders if there are perhaps 3000 chambers in the lab that she's in. It seems absurd, but not impossible. But how is it that the tables have turned, and humans have captured 3000 extra-terrestrials here? She moves slower now, the question begging for her attention.

She stops again and moves to the front of a chamber, looking inside it. She looks at the being in the coffin, at rest, waiting. Waiting? She asks herself what they could possibly be waiting for if indeed that is what they are doing.

Alexis looks again at the label on the bottom of the chamber. She reads it over and over, thinking back to all the research she did herself. Her heart is racing, almost as quickly as thoughts and images are flashing through her head. What is going on here, she asks herself out loud.

She knows there must be a logical explanation for this room, but she can't think right now what it could be. She racks her brain, putting all the information that she gathered on her own in as logical a sequence as she can muster. But nothing she comes up with is making any sense. Why can she not make sense of this, now that she is in this room that vindicates and validates all the work she was doing?

The humming sound of the chambers coming to life gets closer to them, and they move on a little further, a little bit closer to the door. She stops again when the humming seems to stop. She notices that it is stopping and starting at regular intervals now, and neither she nor Tucker has the gumption to look and see what is going on in the chambers that have stopped humming now.

. . .

The sterility of the room suddenly gets to them, as the chambers they're in front of him to life. The two watch as gas is first pumped into the coffin, and then they watch as the liquid drains out of it. One pipe seems to lead the liquid away, into a large tank beside each chamber. Gas is then pumped in from another large tank, through the pipes that seem to be connected to the being inside.

When the eyes of the alien they're looking at suddenly open the pair scurry for cover. There's no real place to hide except for behind the chamber between the two large tanks. They don't know if they've been seen or even if the being inside knows what it is looking at.

From behind her chamber, Alexis looks over to Tucker, who is behind the chamber just next to her. He is practically plastered to the wall, not wanting to touch the chamber, obviously regretting coming in here in the first place. But then he braves it and goes around for a look at the alien contained in his chamber. Its eyes are also opening, a slow blinking, like somebody that has just woken from the deepest sleep.

Again Tucker and Alexis are in the crawlspace behind the chambers, separated by the large tanks extracting liquid and pumping gas into the chamber. They look at each other without speaking, scared that the aliens might hear them now. The questions that each of them has mix with the fear in their eyes and their faces tighten. Tucker tells himself to be composed, to breathe, Alexis is practically hyperventilating, with fear, anxiety, excitement.

· · ·

Tucker checks his weapon; he checks that it is loaded and that the safety is off. If any one of these beings decides to make a move, he will be ready for it. If they all decided to make a move, he will not be as ready. He looks at the door in the distance, and it suddenly seems like its miles away from where they are.

Alexis looks like she needs to be held, and so Tucker squeezes himself between the tanks to get to her. He places an arm around her and pulls her closer to him, but it's difficult, the space behind the chambers really cramped. But just having contact with her, holding her, is enough for him. It seems to comfort him too.

They wait, not sure of what will happen next. They watch, as far as the eye can see, as the chambers drain of their liquid. Then the slow and steady pumping of gas resumes, at a slightly escalated rate. Still, they wait, unable to move, still uncertain about what is going on, or what will happen next.

Then the activity in every chamber that they can see stops. They listen for anything, but nothing. Alexis seems to have calmed down now, Tucker too. The silence in the room is eerie but strangely comforting. But still, they cannot move, even though the door is in sight.

"We should probably..." Tucker starts.

"No, wait...just wait." Alexis isn't ready to move. Being in such close proximity to Tucker makes her feel safe suddenly as if moving will somehow separate them and she will lose this feeling.

Tucker just keeps holding her, knowing that this is what

she needs, what she wants. He tries to pull her closer but it's just too cramped behind the chambers. So they just stand there, half embracing, half not, looking at each other and at the door that will get them away from these aliens.

Alexis inhales deeply several times. And then she starts to move, slowly, not wanting to be separated from Tucker. But it really is an uncomfortable squeeze behind the coffins, and after breathing in deeply Alexis makes her way out of the crawlspace. Tucker follows, holding her better when they are again between the coffins.

She walks slowly, looking at the aliens now, as they open their eyes. But the stare is blank, and so they know that the aliens are not looking at them. The beings seem to be orienting themselves in the absence of the liquid, but it doesn't look uncomfortable. In fact, it looks too comfortable, as though their presence here is insignificant. They stop and look directly at one of the aliens. Suddenly it seems to look back, to stare at them, through them, and they freeze.

The alien seems to look from Tucker to Alexis, and back again. It seems to look at the gun in Tucker's hand, which he can't help but point directly at it. But then it returns to its blank staring, seemingly unconcerned for what is going on outside of the coffin. Tucker's finger is on the trigger, ready to squeeze it if the alien made a threatening move. Actually, if it moved at all, he would probably fire.

After the longest pause, Tucker relaxes his stance, going back to holding Alexis, who is proving to be as safe a place for him as he is for her. Alexis seems to be planted in one place now, on the spot, so that Tucker has to nudge her along. Still, she won't move. She suddenly has one clear question on her mind. What was Chloe doing in this room? And why did the World Government feel that they could trust her with this, and not Alexis? Why did Grant Chambers go to Chloe with this?

She asks this question out loud, no longer worried about waking the aliens. They're already awake, sort of. She half expects Tucker to answer her because she looks at him when she asks the question again. Tucker's blank stare lets her know that he doesn't have the answers she's looking for. How could he know? He's been with her the whole time, and he's been as surprised as she has been at each discovery.

The question causes her forehead to furrow. 'Think Alexis, think', she tells herself. Tucker just wants to get them out of the room, but Alexis refuses to move. Why Chloe? The question now burns her insides like bad whisky, and she feels like she might throw up.

Perhaps it's because they didn't trust her to begin with. But then why hire her as head of archeology, and not Chloe? Or perhaps it's the research she's been doing? But she hasn't neglected any of her duties to the World Government. She reminds herself that she was just getting all the facts, all her ducks in a row before she approached them with her findings. Would her research have led her here, to this room, though, had the lab not exploded, she wonders?

The door hisses suddenly, and Tucker and Alexis look from one another to the door. They squeeze themselves in the crawlspace again, separating them. In the silence of the room, they hear every lever, every gear engaging in the complicated mechanism. The chambers suddenly feel see-through, as if anyone who came into the room would spot them immediately. Still, they hide as best they can.

From their vantage point, thirty or so chambers deep, they can see Chloe. She comes in and out of focus, as she passes the chambers, nonchalant. They look at one another again but say nothing. Then they return their stare towards the center of the room, which is quickly filling up with another shipment of refugees. Different ones, if Alexis's memory serves her well. Tucker just watches his sister.

A moment later the door hisses again, back onto its hinges, and is shut. The pair watches as the humans, seemingly in a trance, are lined up by the guards in the room. Not security guards from the many checkpoints mind you, these are a different breed altogether. Tucker struggles to get to his badge, eventually getting it out of its holder on his belt. There really is hardly any space to move where they're at.

They watch these silent, stunned humans, who look like they either can't speak English or just won't. They watch how they are lined up by the guards, each one placed just so. It looks like a very elaborate chess game, and these people are the pawns. Questions start to buzz around Alexis's head again, but she tells herself that the answer will be delivered quickly. These guys seem to be just too out of it to lift or move anything. Then what are they here for?

A thought settles over Alexis and she has to stop herself from screaming. What if they are food for the aliens? I mean, what else would these aliens eat here on earth, a planet that can barely sustain them for longer than a few days or hours if the labels on their coffins are anything to go by?

Tucker just keeps his eye on his sister, who is like a choirmaster, a chess master of sorts, making sure that each of the humans is perfectly placed. He also watches the guards, who are armed. He knows that his badge will have little effect on them somehow. He just knows it. But all he has is his badge, his service pistol no match for the fire he will come under if there is a shootout.

Alexis counts a hundred humans, most of them still to the side. But she counts about a hundred people now perfectly lined up. The humans just stare blankly in front of them, and Alexis wonders if they even know what is going on, or what is about to happen to them.

She watches Chloe giving instructions to the guards, but strains to hear what she is saying. The room seems to echo with the sound of her voice, but no words can be made out. She sounds remarkably composed, Alexis thinks, if she is about to feed these humans to the aliens. Alexis can't help it, she edges closer to Chloe, desperate for a clearer view, and desperate to hear what she has to say.

"Which ones, sir," Chloe speaks into her mobile phone. "Alright, got it!" She hangs up. Alexis wishes that she could hear who she was speaking to, but she thinks she knows. It can only be Grant Chambers.

· · ·

The chambers suddenly lift out of sockets in the floor, their tanks too. Not all of them mind you, but the entire row, about five rows from where Alexis is standing, Tucker armed and next to her, begins to move. It is like an automated chessboard, and these chambers swop with the ones in front. She looks around, anticipating movements from the chambers that they are behind. When nothing happens she returns her stare to the center of the room.

Chloe is on her mobile phone again. "Yes Mr. Chambers, yes sir." This confirms what Alexis already knew. But what is she confirming to Grant Chambers? What knowledge is shared between the two of them? Again Alexis wishes that she knew what Grant was saying on the other end. But even her hearing isn't that good.

She looks at Tucker, a 'what next' look on her face. Tucker shoots back with an 'I really have no idea' look. They just stare at each other for a while. But then the chambers in the front are humming again, and both of them look in the direction that this humming is coming from.

They move closer still, close enough to see inside the front chambers now. Through the glass, they can make out that the tubes entering the extra-terrestrials come off with a loud hiss. The beings inside seem to exhale. And then the lids come off each chamber and Alexis has to stop herself from making a sound, although what she wants to do is scream at Chloe for not knowing what she is doing.

There is movement in the chambers now, and so Alexis's attention shifts to the inside of one in particular. She keeps checking that Tucker is looking at the same thing. He must be because his gun now hangs in his hand like a toy pistol. The look on his face is one of absolute shock so that Alexis feels like slapping him, just to bring him back to the moment, where this is really happening.

One by one the aliens exit the chambers. They stretch like they've been sleeping deeply for a long time. Alexis watches as each extra-terrestrial exits its chamber and walks up to the rows of humans. She holds her breath, not sure what she even expects to happen next, but knowing that she is not ready for it, whatever it is. She hides a little further behind the tank that she is standing next to, pulling Tucker with her because he is all but standing out in the open now.

They watch as the aliens seem to inspect the human beings. Some of the more tentacled ones look like they might just take a bite out of the subject in front of them. Thinking of these people, these human beings, as subjects, seems strange and overwhelming, yet rather accurate. The humans are just motionless, putty in the aliens' hands, or their tentacles, depending on which being is examining you.

Chloe moves through them, and for a minute she too doesn't look human. What kind of research is going on here, what experiment is being carried out? Alexis wonders this as she moves in for a closer look. But Tucker has returned to his senses now, and so he pulls her back behind the tank. Hours seem to drift seamlessly by as the two observe this ritual-like examination of human beings.

. . .

Then Chloe is on the phone again. No prize for guessing who she is speaking to. The conversation sounds like it is being had in a tin, everything now a haze to Alexis. What she does make out is that 'the shipment is acceptable.' But what shipment is she talking about?

Then the first row of humans move forward, guided by aliens and guards alike, Chloe merely observing. They all watch as the people step into the chambers, replacing the aliens that were just a few minutes ago contained there. They move like robots, animated yet not. They all still have a blank expression on their faces, as if they are just going through the motions. Alexis and Tucker watch this movement with interest, wondering what could possibly be going on now.

The aliens seem stronger now as if they have settled into the earth's atmosphere. As Alexis and Tucker watch on, the chambers close, each person perfectly fitting in the coffins, as if they were designed for them. Alexis wonders again what could be going on since she expected a mass-feeding frenzy to say the least. But nothing of the sort happens. The humans just replace the aliens in the coffins, and now the coffins are closed.

Then the chambers hum to life and the pair behind the tanks is once again spellbound. All this excitement is proving to be much more than either of them expected. They watch as the tubes that were connected to the aliens are now connected to the humans, piercing their necks, and one seeming to enter their chests. Alexis gasps, thinking that there is no way that the humans could survive this penetrative violation. And to make matters worse, the chambers are now starting to fill with the same murky liquid that housed the aliens, so that Alexis thinks that they might drown.

But nothing of the sort happens. The humans are as calm and docile as before, with no wild lashing and thrashing about like one would expect from a drowning person. It seems like a very elaborate suicide, but not really. Alexis wishes that she could see their faces, but she has to be content with the view from the back.

Gas is pumped into the humans, at a slow and steady pace. Everything seems to be happening in slow motion. But when they check their watches, they've been in the room for less than two hours. It's actually all very surreal. They feel like they're watching a science-fiction film in 3D!

The humans inside the chambers are suddenly animated. Not wildly so, but they seem to be reaching out and touching the glass now, as if they are curious about the outside world suddenly, as if the world outside their heads is suddenly coming into view. They've been submersed in the liquid now for longer than ten minutes, but still no sign of drowning. The gas just pumps steadily through them, and they relax again after a while, just lying there, letting the gas flow through them.

A word settles in Alexis's head: preparation. That is what it seems is happening. The humans seem to be being prepared for something, but what? She wishes that she could get a closer look, but if they moved any closer to the action, they will definitely be seen. So they just stay put behind the tank, beside it, and observe.

The chambers continue to hum, and then a draining sound fills the room. They watch as the liquid drains out of the chambers now, and almost expect that the humans will slump forward. But they seem to be as strong as ever, breathing now with the assistance of these tubes, and definitely not breathing oxygen.

Then the chambers mist up in the absence of the liquid. Alexis isn't sure, but they seem to be drying out. Alexis almost thinks that it might have been easier if these humans were naked. But then the mist clears, and all you can hear is the gas pumps at work.

Then suddenly the humans contained in the chambers start to 'fade!' Is '*fade*' even the word that she would use to describe what is happening, she isn't sure. But that is the only one that comes to mind. The humans inside the chambers move in and out of focus, like the way TVs used to so that you had to hit them on the side to bring them back into focus. Alexis almost wants to hit the side of the chamber, so that the human inside it doesn't completely disappear.

But then they do, leaving the tubes dangling in the chamber that is again filling with liquid. But it drains almost as quickly as it fills. Then the mist that seems to serve no purpose other than to dry the inside of the coffin, or to disinfect it. Whatever it is doing, it does it quickly. And then the chambers fill again with human beings and the whole exercise is repeated.

. . .

"Teleportation?!" Alexis whispers to Tucker, but it's more like she mouths the word. She had always thought that this was just a gimmick, a mode of transportation made up for the movies, the stuff of fairytales. But right in front of her, human beings are being teleported to...where?

Tucker is glued to the inside of his chamber, the one that he has chosen as his focal point out of the hundred or so that have moved. He doesn't even register that Alexis is trying to speak with him, or if he does, it definitely doesn't show on his face.

Alexis returns to watching this, and she questions herself again. Perhaps these humans are simply disintegrating into the chambers, to provide the necessary sustenance for the aliens when they return to their sarcophagi. But she knows somehow that she is right. To question herself, after all, she's witnessed is at best stupid.

When it's just Chloe, the aliens, and the guards left in the room Chloe is once again on the phone, confirming that all went well and that the humans have been successfully transported to various colonies across many galaxies. After the call she hangs up and turns to the aliens, not communicating with them, but in as much awe of these beings as one would expect her to be.

She seems to be examining these beings now, checking that everything is okay with them, as a doctor might examine a patient. But what could she possibly know about extraterrestrial life, and how quickly did she learn their physiology? Chloe is obviously far more ambitious than Alexis had anticipated, and her ambition seems to have gotten her somewhere with Grant Chambers.

Alexis suddenly remembers Zach, and how Chloe seduced the young man. She thinks of her filing cabinet, and one and one makes two. She tries to remember everything that was contained in the file marked Miscellaneous. She knows that the combination of these factors came together to bring them to this point where she is no longer trusted by the World Government.

She also knows that she would never have agreed to this, so that is why they probably never asked her. She wonders how many of the world's leaders are aware that America is stockpiling aliens, or that human beings are being intergalactically trafficked. She wonders a lot of things, but only to herself. Alexis can't bring herself to articulate any of the questions in her head, partly because there are so many, and partly because the room is now a deathly silence. She will ask these questions once they get out of here, and are safely away from the World Government and its shenanigans.

CHAPTER 9

THE SECONDS GO by like hours, and there is no sign that the aliens are going to be put back in their chambers. Something in the air must have them riled up because they look around wildly. But Alexis notices that it's not that they're being wild, it's just that they appear wilder the longer they are exposed to the earth's atmosphere.

It's too warm for them, and soon enough they're getting back in their coffins. Alexis wants to see everything, but she can't bring herself to look when the alien behind whose coffin she is hiding gets inside. She hadn't realized that she and Tucker had come so far forward. She doesn't see the pipes attach themselves to the being as the chamber fills with an icy liquid. Then the pipes pump gas into the alien, and through the chamber so that a few gas bubbles escape through its mouth and nose before the entire system settles and it appears that the alien has gone to sleep again.

. . .

The entire lab goes dark once all the aliens are safe inside their chambers. So Alexis was actually right, and aliens have come to earth with a sinister motive. But how do they keep these humans alive in outer space, if they themselves cannot survive for very long without the chambers? It seems an awful amount of effort for nothing. But she will worry about that later. Right now, they need to get out of here.

"Okay, that's the last one," Chloe says, looking very proud of herself.

"Very good my dear, I knew you would be a better fit than your predecessor, given the delicate nature of our work here." Grant Chambers is on speaker now so that Chloe can finish up while talking to him. He sounds smug, already having dismissed Alexis in his head, before even letting her know. She finds it strange that she was even allowed into the building, since it's quite obvious that Chloe now has her job. Or maybe this is just a special assignment, one that she would not have been fit for, especially given her research.

Anyway, she will think about this later, once they've cleared the building. But just in case they don't get another chance to be in here, she takes out her phone, and takes a few more pictures. This will make for one hell of a story once the papers get a hold of it. But something still doesn't feel right, and so for now, Alexis decides that only she and Tucker need to know what is going on here. She does feel an added sense of urgency though, almost as though she needs to figure this thing out once and for all before someone she knows is sent to god knows where for god knows what. She suddenly wishes that there was a god she could turn to who would make it better; make all this seem like a very bad dream.

Thankfully the lab opens from the inside, and soon enough Alexis and Tucker are free from the visuals of extra-terrestrials. It seemed like Chloe and her cronies would never leave. They go to the old lab, and look around, giving everything the once over once more. Again Alexis takes out her cell, and again she is taking pictures of every corner of the vast space. Her office no longer has a floor, the ceiling of the lab bringing it down with it during the explosion. But she manages to get some good shots.

They make for the stairwell, and the security guard looks at them as though they appeared from nowhere. It's not the same guard as before so they know they will probably have some explaining to do. Fortunately, the guards trust each other, or they're just too lazy to do their work and therefore assume that the one before them has done his job, so soon Alexis and Tucker are making for the outside of the building. It's almost 1 AM.

Tucker and Alexis give it a minute before they too make for the outside world, heading to where Tucker parked his car. It's there thankfully. Alexis really is becoming more and more paranoid as the days go by. Tucker drives straight home without even thinking to ask Alexis if she wouldn't perhaps like to be dropped at her place.

Tucker is totally paranoid now, locking and relocking the front door, something he has never done before. As long as he had his weapon at hand, he had always felt safe. Now, the whole world had gone mad, and everything he once believed about humanity has been turned on its head.

Alexis goes into a downstairs bathroom and washes her face. She washes her neck too, somehow needing to get the feeling that something is crawling on her. It doesn't work, and after three tries she exits the bathroom, towel still in hand, dabbing her face dry.

She walks out into Tucker, who has two drinks in his hand. For tonight, or rather this morning, the growl in his stomach will have to wait. He is torn, visibly. Could he have done anything to stop the humans from being teleported away to some cold and distant place? Should he have just called for backup?

Alexis takes one of the drinks and goes towards the closest fire, in an informal lounging area downstairs. She settles on the rug in front of the hearth and stares at the flames. This house seems to be run by invisible forces, people that you never see, only ever seeing the result of their efforts.

Tucker stands behind her, drink in one hand, and the bottle in the other. Tonight was really too much for him, and the more he thinks about it, the more it freaks him out. What is he going to do about this is the question uppermost in his mind. He knows that he needs to do something.

"What are we going to do about this?" Alexis asks the question that is itching at Tucker's scalp.

· · ·

"I don't know yet, but I'll think of something," Tucker answers her honestly, really not sure about what he is going to do about this, uncertain about what he will tell his own bosses about this, not sure how much, if anything, they know about what is going on at the World Government.

He fills her glass with a whisky that rivals even the bottle she got from Grant, and again she is reminded of where she is. Alexis can't help but think back to a time when this house was complete, with mother and father, two children who were probably destined for great things in their youth, but who went off and did exactly what they wanted. She can imagine Tucker and Chloe running their father's business, had they been so inclined. But that would have meant that she wouldn't be sitting here right now, in this house, with this would-be businessman turned detective. She keeps her gratitude for the way things worked out to herself, but can't help breathing a sigh of huge relief.

Tucker joins her on the rug, sitting behind her and beside her all at once. He seems to be all over her without touching her. She wants him to touch her, to hold her so that all that has happened will melt away into him. But he is careful, still occupied by his own take on events.

She turns to him, putting her glass down at the same time. She goes up to him and kisses him with her eyes open, wanting to see his response. His eyes are also open, but he obviously wants to kiss her, the passion dripping from his lips. Then both their eyes close simultaneously, and the kiss goes to that place where they are both lost to one another yet present, their lips parting just long enough for them to breathe. They go down so that they are now lying side by side, facing one another, joined at the lips, but aching to be joined elsewhere, more completely.

Tucker's hands are on her now, touching her with an intensity that borders on too much. He's waited too long for this moment. But Alexis isn't complaining, and she is not about to. As his fingertips create grooves up her legs she closes them, but only for a moment, and only as a reflex. She wants him with every fiber of her being.

She wishes that she was out of her clothes already, but does nothing to make this happen. She can't rush this, she can't rush him. He knows what she wants, and what he wants. They want the same thing. But Tucker will have to take the reigns on this ride, just in case, Alexis scares the horse that is about to mount her.

He holds her head up with one hand, the other making several tracks up and down her legs, over her jeans. She wishes that he would just take them off already. She reminds herself that this can't be rushed, not sure if she wants him, or just sex. It's this conflict that allows her to step back, just until he has worked her over enough for the answer not to matter.

When Tucker finally goes for the button on her jeans she feels like she is going to explode. He releases it carefully, checking her face for confirmation that this is okay. It is, and so he makes slow work of her zip, just until this confirmation settles over him. But she is lying on her back now, instructing him with her eyes that it's okay for him to remove her pants. He does just that.

· · ·

He goes to work on his own pants before she has to take over, he has forgotten that he is wearing a belt. She helps him out of his jeans and drops them next to hers on the floor. Tucker isn't wearing any underwear, and Alexis looks at his nakedness for a moment, processing it, hoping that she hasn't bitten off more than she can chew. But he'll be gentle, she knows this. She trusts him.

It's not like she's a virgin anyway. But she's had more sex with herself than anyone else since she started working at the World Government, and she suddenly wishes she got out more. But she needs this, he needs this. So they resume their kissing in between taking each other's tops off. When they are both naked they settle back down on the rug and take their kissing to the next level.

Tucker makes sure that Alexis is ready to receive him, really ready. And when he enters her she moans loudly, for no other reason than that it is exactly as she imagined it would be. It's perfect!

"Are you okay," Tucker checks. He has too, realizing their difference in size.

"Yes, I'm fine..." Alexis gasps, each stroke tenderer than the one before it so that soon there is no need for them to speak. They are lost in the art of lovemaking now, and for a while at least, the events of the last while evaporate into nothing. They make love until the sun comes up and then sleep for half the day. They make love again twice before they bathe, where they make love again. Alexis wishes that her life was simple now, fully understanding the simple pleasures that can be exchanged between a man and a woman.

Over dinner, take out again, and wine, they discuss finally the scene from the previous night. It's not a subdued discussion mind you, both of them very vocal on the matter of aliens trafficking human beings.

"Perhaps they're prisoners, lifers, you know. Really bad men who have no place on earth anymore? And god knows how overcrowded our prison system is." Tucker tries for a logical explanation that will not completely deface the World Government. He has to believe in our leadership. If not, then what do we have really?

"I don't think so, Tucker. They looked scared, really scared. And some of them were so young!" Alexis tries to remember the faces of the men that were beamed to somewhere else right in front of her. She can't, not a single face comes to mind so that what she has just said makes no more sense to her.

"The question is why though, if not to another penal colony. Why would our government be giving humans to the aliens?" Tucker takes a sip from his wine, astounded by how casually the word 'aliens' now rolls off his tongue.

"That is the million-dollar question. That's what we need to find out, soon!" Again Alexis emphasizes the urgency of everything that is happening. She looks at Tucker, who is looking at her now with different eyes. He knows her now, really knows her. And he likes it.

. . .

They decide that it can wait until tomorrow before they go to the World Government. But one thing is clear, whatever they find out when they get there, it won't be pretty. Tucker considers calling in reinforcements. He thinks better of it though and goes to get another bottle of wine from his cellar. He is grateful now that his father was such an avid collector of wines.

This bottle they take to the bedroom. It's Alexis's first time in his bedroom and she is suddenly nervous, almost as though the last few hours didn't happen at all. When they make love on Tucker's bed it's beautiful. It feels like the first time all over again, and she is in heaven. Him too and both of them don't even need to say this to each other. It's written all over their faces.

They make love throughout the night, as if they might disappear come morning, or as if this is going to all turn out to be a dream. If it is a dream, it is one that neither of them wants to wake from, ever. When they eventually fall asleep it's in each other's arms. Alexis has never been as comfortable with a man before. And Tucker has never wanted to give a woman his everything before. They have definitely crossed the line between making out and being in a relationship now. And neither of them wants to go back over it.

They arrive at the World Government's headquarters just before nine AM the next morning. Alexis recognizes the guards at the first checkpoint and has a conversation with them. She goes in with her finger, just to see if it will work. She knows it won't. And now she knows why.

She tries her retinal scan, but this won't work either, the retinal scan dependant of her fingerprint getting her past the first stage of security. She tries her finger again. And again the scan buzzes a deep red, flashing 'unauthorized' in black. She looks at the guard, who eyes her and Tucker suspiciously now. And why wouldn't he, he's just doing his job. They have no choice, Tucker flashing his badge confidently so that they are let through.

"We're here to see Grant Chambers," Tucker says to the first security guard in the building. He lifts his badge so that the guy behind the counter with the magazine he was reading hidden knows that he's serious.

"You can't just come in here and demand to see the president. That's not exactly how it works." The security guard is not speaking from experience, since nobody had ever dared just march into headquarters and demand a sitting with the president.

"Oh I think this says I can," Tucker retorts, pointing to his badge. But he knows that this really has no weight here, so he is really taking a chance. If that was the case, any cop with a gripe with the president could just march up to his office and put a bullet in his head.

. . .

The security guard looks at Tucker and his badge with mild disdain. He knows what the rules say at the World Government, and he knows the procedures that need to be followed before one meets with the president. These rules are more lax if you actually work in the building, but Tucker doesn't work here, and Alexis probably doesn't work here anymore.

"I think he'll want to see me," Alexis interjects. She looks from Tucker to the security guard, feeling uncertain of herself but knowing that she needs to get in and see Grant Chambers.

The security guard excuses himself and then picks up the phone in front of him. He turns away, as though they would suddenly be unable to hear him if he has his back to them. The conversation lasts a little less than ten seconds, and then he turns back on his chair so that he is facing them again. "You're going to have to leave that here," he says, eyeing Tucker's gun.

"I'll hold on to it, if it's all the same to you," Tucker doesn't understand why today they want him to leave his pistol at the desk when he's been in this building several times with it.

"Then you're going to have to stay down here with it, ma'am, you can go through." The guard is not going to budge on this, and Tucker has played 'chicken' enough times to know when someone isn't bluffing. He reasons that since he will be going up to see the president, that he be unarmed is not an altogether unreasonable request. Reluctantly, he hands the guard his weapon.

Alexis must be off the database because they have to process her from scratch. Fingerprint, one entry, one exit; Tucker too. This will get them up the elevator to the president's office, and back down to this foyer. They will need to be let out through the security checkpoints by a guard.

It feels like a real slap in the face, almost as though she was being processed downtown; Alexis feels violated. To think how smug she was in this very building just a few weeks earlier, and now she has to enter it with a visitor's lapel. And all this without being told by her bosses that she was fired. She starts to get worked up, thinking of the million things she has to say to Grant Chambers.

The ride up the elevator seems slow, painfully so. But Alexis has too much on her mind to engage with Tucker in any meaningful way. She just looks at her hands, crossing her fingers over each other like a naughty child who's been sent to see the principal. But she hasn't come to see the principal. She has come to see the president of the entire world to discuss a matter of the utmost importance. And she isn't in the wrong here, she keeps reminding herself. It isn't her who is trafficking human beings.

The elevator opens, and the chill hits them like a forceful wind. Alexis immediately wraps her coat tighter around herself. Grant Chambers is wearing shorts, predictably, but it really is nippy inside the large space. Alexis realizes that it is not that there is no air-conditioning, but that the air-conditioning has been set really low.

. . .

"Come in my dear, come in," Grant is his usual chirpy self. Tucker looks at his legs, exposed to the cold as they are, and then he throws Alexis a 'what the hell' look. She shoots back with a 'don't ask'.

"We need to talk," Alexis says, already looking to where Grant is pouring the scotch. She needs it for reasons other than the cold this morning. Tucker has a question mark on his face. Alexis notices this, and just mouths 'drink' to him. He does as he is told.

"Yes, we do. But first, what is on your mind, my dear?" Grant offers them the drinks and watches over the rim of his glass as they take huge gulps from the liquid. The scotch takes a minute to settle into the places inside the couple that it needs to in order for them to relax.

"I know about the room downstairs, is that why I've been fired?" Alexis goes in for the kill immediately. She sees no need to be polite or to skirt the issue with him. Tucker just stands back and lets her handle the situation. She's obviously been here before, and she seems to have something on her mind that really can't wait.

"There you go, jumping to conclusions again my dear, so quick," Grant is composed as he sniffs the contents of his glass.

"What conclusion am I supposed to have come to, sir," Alexis doesn't forget who she's speaking with.

"Perhaps we just thought that the assignment was beyond your skillset that is all, my dear!"

Alexis wants to scream at him for many reasons, but mostly because he insists on ending every sentence with 'my dear.'

She almost can't stand it now, especially given the events of the last couple of days. She feels like anything but 'dear' to this man with his shorts on in his wintry office.

"And just what skills exactly are required to traffic human beings to some unknown and lonely place?" Alexis feels the anger inside her well up like heartburn. She just wants to grab Grant Chambers by the throat and scream 'you can't do that.' But she restrains herself, trusting that the question carries sufficient clout.

"Well, firstly. You still have a job here; we just need to get the lab sorted out." Grant looks away from her for the first time when he says this so that Alexis knows that it isn't altogether true. She watches him suspiciously now, as though at any minute he might just blurt out the truth about what is actually going on downstairs. He doesn't. And so she returns momentarily to her scotch.

"Why don't I believe you," she asks him, eventually, the scotch hugging her tightly now so that she feels safe in its warm embrace. There is a stare down for the longest time so that Tucker searches his head for something, anything that might break the deathly silence.

After the silence, it's clear that Grant isn't going to say anything that is going to break the stalemate. He walks up to the doors that Alexis knows to open up into the board-room, although she has only ever accessed this room via the elevator. Grant Chambers looks like he is searching his head for something to say, something that will placate her, but he comes up short. Eventually, he just pushes the doors open, and turns to them with a look that says 'follow me.' They finish the remainder of the whisky in their glasses as they get up and follow him into the chilly boardroom, as dark and creepy as the lab downstairs now, Alexis thinks.

Grant paces this room too, looking like a cornered lion. He looks like he wants to say something, but just doesn't know what. Alexis eyes him with passive aggression that has Tucker wishing he had insisted on bringing his pistol up to the penthouse. Grant Chambers could easily have them disposed of, and nobody would be any wiser. He places a hand over where his gun should be, suddenly regretting its absence.

"What's this about sir," Alexis asks, wanting to ask him something else but not sure yet how to articulate it.

"Just wait, my dear, patience please!" There is a hint of anxiety in Grant's voice that unsettles even Alexis now, and she looks to where Tucker's gun was, his hand still over the place on his belt that housed it.

"I just want to know if I still have a job here, and what the hell is going on downstairs." She wants to threaten him with a massive exposure in the press, but thinks better of it, knowing that this is not the time for threats. After all, Grant might still say something to redeem himself, something that will make this whole mess make some sort of sense. Right now, any sense will do.

Grant is silent now, as he turns on the many screens around the room. China and Brazil are in view, seated behind their elaborate desks. Alexis thinks that this is strange, given that these two places are in opposing time zones, but she doesn't say anything. Soon enough though, more of the world's leaders take their place in front of the cameras that must be right in front of them. They look directly at the camera as if Grant Chambers is about to say something of the utmost importance.

"She knows," is all Grant says when he has the attention of the world's leaders. They look around at each other so that you get the feeling again that they are all in the same room somewhere.

"Knows what exactly," Africa asks, needing clarity.

"Everything," is all Grant Chambers says, although Alexis has a million unanswered questions.

It seems like all their eyes suddenly fall on Alexis, and she gets a cold shiver, one that has nothing to do with the temperature in the room. Again she looks at Tucker as if staring at the place where his gun should be will make it magically appear. She feels threatened suddenly, by these faces staring at her through the screen, even though the people on the other end are a million miles away, give or take.

"And who is this," Russia asks, obviously referring to Tucker. Tucker suddenly puts his hands behind his back, like a reprimanded schoolboy. He can't think of anything else to do with his hands. He isn't sure if he should intro-duce himself.

"A policeman," is Grant's casual response. He looks at Tucker for a name, but this isn't forthcoming. So Grant asks him to introduce himself. He does, emphasizing that he is a detective with the New York police department. But these words seem to just bounce off the screens like a screensaver, mildly irritating Russia and Australia.

"Oh," is all he gets in response, and he knows that his title carries no weight with these leaders. He is suddenly anxious, feeling like he's walked straight into an ambush, one that he saw coming but couldn't stop himself, like a moth to a flame. He straightens himself up unnecessarily, trying to make himself taller than he already is.

"This body was getting a little uncomfortable..." Grant says, letting the sentence settle over his audience now, so that Alexis looks from Tucker to Grant Chambers, and then around at the world leaders on each screen, wondering why none of them seem surprised by what she thinks Grant is saying.

"Oh relax Grant, you'll be out of there soon enough, and back on your own planet. We just need to find a suitable presidential candidate first, one that understands the importance of our work on earth!" China is really annoyed now that it seems that Grant Chambers is letting every cat out of the bag.

"One that's preferably human. How does any species even survive on this planet?" Grant has now officially excused himself from the human race. Alexis almost expects him to pull back his face to reveal a hideous creature underneath the flesh that covers it. But no such luck. That explains why the office was kept so cold, why he always wore shorts, why he hasn't made a public appearance in forever, and why he only sniffs his scotch, never drinking it. It must be very cold in outer space, she thinks.

Alexis and Tucker look at the screens now, wondering just how many of the faces staring at them are actually human. None of them, it seems, from the ensuing conversation. They wonder how long this has been going on, that the world has been run by aliens, and seemingly with the help of humans themselves.

"It was the best way to do it," Grant half-answers her question.

"Do what exactly," Alexis steels herself against whatever response she might get, knowing now that she isn't speaking to a human being.

"We have needs that are best serviced by humans, elsewhere, and instead of taking over the planet outright, and inciting a revolution, we decided to do it this way. We also had to be sure that you would keep on breeding. Cloning is such a tedious process." Again Grant Chambers speaks in riddles, Alexis having to read between the lines. Tucker is too flabbergasted to say anything. Again he goes for his gun, which isn't there.

"So I take it we won't leave this room then," Alexis finally asking what is on Tucker's mind.

"There you go jumping to conclusions again my dear," Grant has regained some of his composure. He looks menacingly at Tucker and Alexis now though, as do the rest of the faces on the screens, and it is clear that none of the faces appearing on the screens like where Grant Chambers is going to go with this.

"So you're gonna just let us walk out of here, after what we know?" Tucker needs confirmation of what Chambers, or whatever he is, is saying.

"Yes, you will walk out of here my dear, and you will go about your business as usual. You, my dear, will wait until we are ready for you to return to your duties as head of archeology." Alexis isn't sure anymore about Grant's 'my dears'. It seems to have been something that someone taught him to say, probably when they were preparing him to take over Grant's body. She feels like telling him that the reference doesn't mean as much when you say it to a man, but she decides to keep this to herself, Tucker not noticing it at all.

"And what if we can't just walk out of here and go about our business, what if we take this to the papers, and tell the whole world what you're up to here?" Alexis again asks the question that fails to come out of Tucker's mouth. He seems to be preoccupied examining the human faces of the world's leaders, looking for anything that would give away what they really are.

"Then my dear, I'm afraid you will be responsible, single handedly, for the demise of the human race." Grant lets this settle over the pair as he turns off the screens and then leads them back through the doors that separate this space from his penthouse. He waves at them as they leave, and both of them cannot believe just how human he looks. One thing is clear though, Alexis and Tucker have just placed a very big bulls-eye on their backs, one that neither of them can shake off.

CHAPTER 10

THE EXPLOSION RIPS through the house like a ninja. Three explosions and the house falls into its foundation, like it never was. Tucker is at the gym trying to work through things in his head when he gets the call from the fire department, and he rushes home.

Four stories have been reduced to dust. All that is left of the massive structure are the steel beams that held it up, now protruding out of the earth like an acupuncturist's needles. There isn't even any smoke when he arrives at the house, clearly the work of an expert.

"Was there anybody in the house sir?" the question sounds like it's being asked in the distance, to someone else. Tucker just looks at what is left of his home and shakes his head in disbelief.

"Is that a 'no' sir, please, we need to know," the question still sounding distant.

"No, there was nobody in the house, nobody except the guy responsible for this." Tucker is angry and anxious all at the same time, not knowing what to make of this, but knowing that it definitely has something to do with Alexis, and the work they're doing; and knowing that it definitely has something to do with Grant Chambers.

"It was probably detonated remotely, sir. It seems to have been a rather complicated contraption, just the house was damaged." The fire chief tries to make this sound like it's some sort of consolation.

"Destroyed, the house has been completely destroyed. Or am I not looking at the same thing you are?" Tucker takes his anger out on the wrong person.

"I'm sorry sir, but at least nobody was hurt. At least there's that." Again the fire chief makes it sound like what he's saying is supposed to make Tucker feel better for having lost his family home.

"Excuse me, I need to make a phone call," he says, excusing himself and dialing the number at the same time. "Hello, Alexis, they've just blown up my house." He states this as a matter of fact and Alexis is silent on the other end, not knowing what to say. "Alexis, are you there?" he asks after it seems like he's lost her.

"Yes, I'm sorry." This is all she can manage, knowing that it's her fault for involving him in the first place.

"Don't be, there's no time for that. Get out onto the street, I'll come and get you." Tucker gives her instructions as he walks to his car, leaving the fire chief to do his job, whatever that is given the total destruction that has taken place here.

"Why?" Alexis asks, assuming that Tucker would want to come to her apartment now that he doesn't have a home.

"Just do it. I think they're trying to get rid of us, and with the explosions rocking New York City recently, it's not a bad idea to have us simply blow up." His reference to them blowing up has Alexis on her feet. She thinks of packing a few things but then thinks better of it. She grabs her laptop and purse and makes for the outside of her building. In the street she doesn't even look around her, just creating as much distance between her and the building as possible.

She wonders if she shouldn't have warned the other tenants, but that would have taken too long. Perhaps she should have let the security guys downstairs know what was up, but would they have believed her. She has cleared three blocks when she sees Tucker's car. And as she gets in, a loud crashing sound comes from behind her. She doesn't even need to look back to know that her building has just gone down in a massive explosion that probably left nothing but the foundation filled with the rubble of twenty stories collapsing in on themselves.

They drive away from the collapsing building, searching for a spot where they can park and regroup. But New York is busy now, the snow completely melted, and more and more pedestrians are on the road. They decide on a motel on the outskirts of the city, paying cash for the night, just in case they're being tracked. They somehow know that they are being tracked, so credit cards are completely out of the question. Even the car they're driving needs to go, but that's a problem for later.

They have nothing but the clothes on their backs, every possession destroyed by the explosions. But Tucker doesn't blame Alexis for what happened. He's glad that she's safe, and that she's here, with him.

Tucker is unable to relax, his mind racing. He needs to report this, and he needs to report it now. He also needs to pick up his bike from the station and leave the car there. If they are indeed tracking them, then he will have a better chance of escaping them on the bike. It's also not in his name yet, since he only recently purchased it. That's one time delaying the paperwork really seems to have worked for him.

He cannot leave Alexis alone; he can't let her out of his sight. So they head for the station on the other side of town. Surely he can get someone to listen to them, just one person who will take the crazy story about aliens trafficking human beings seriously. It takes them almost an hour, but soon enough they're pulling up outside the police station, and headed inside.

They walk inside, past the front desk and immediately they sense that they are being looked at. To be more accurate, they are being gawked at, like you would an accident moments before you had to carry on with your life. But why? Tucker checks to see that they don't have anything on their faces, like mayonnaise, or ketchup. When he sees nothing, he decides that it's just his paranoia getting to him. He had never thought of himself as paranoid until he met

Alexis. Now everything gets to him. It's as if everything is out to get him.

They walk past the desk and the stares, headed in the direction of the station commander's office. He will give them an ear, perhaps two. He and Tucker had always gotten along well, and he had said on more than one occasion that if ever Tucker needed to talk, that his door was always open. Well, now Tucker needs to talk!

As they pass open office doors and an open-plan area, the looks intensify. Nobody greets them, even when Tucker greets first. Something is definitely not right. Tucker can feel it almost as certainly as he feels his gun in its holster. He places his hand on his gun and pulls Alexis closer, not sure what danger they could be in here in the place that you came to in order to escape danger. Still, he isn't sure what's going on, and so he keeps Alexis close to him.

He sees the door to the station commander's office on the other side of the open plan, but suddenly questions going in. If he were inside that office, there would be no escape, no chance of getting away if you needed to get away in a hurry. He lingers in the open plan, hoping that the station commander is in, and hoping that he will appear through the door to his office at any moment.

He does, and the look on his face is off. Nothing about the way he looks at Tucker says 'come and talk to me if you ever need to'. Just then Tucker catches a flash bulletin on the TV in the corner of the room, the same bulletin coming on every

TV in the station. His picture is on the screen, right next to Alexis's, with the word 'WANTED' splashed across their chests. This is bad. Somebody is going through a hell of a lot of effort to make sure that they're caught, and that they will probably 'disappear' in police custody. It's not unheard of for a criminal to 'disappear' after all, at the hands of the boys in blue.

He hears his name come across the room, followed by a 'let's talk in here' that sounds like anything but. Immediately he turns Alexis so that they are now walking in the opposite direction, towards the exit to the building. But this seems to take them forever and a minute and so they pick up the pace.

Suddenly every cop in sight has his hand on his holster, and Tucker is afraid that they might just open fire. But he doesn't stop, knowing that they will be safer in the street. He just keeps them moving until the door thankfully appears in the distance. Two cops walking in to the station catch their picture on the screens and go for their guns. But Tucker is quick on his feet, and the two are brought down with a swiftly executed fist. Then they're on the outside of the building, and on the scooter, leaving the one place that they thought they could go to behind them.

They manage to lose the three cop cars following them, but only just. Tucker slips his motorbike into the motel's parking lot, and parks it near the end between a truck and an SUV, not a great hiding spot if they've already been spotted. Inside the room, Alexis and Tucker try to catch what little breath they have left.

The two of them look at each other for a while, then at the door for longer. They expect a knock at any moment, or a barrage of officers to come storming through at any moment. But when nothing happens for a while, they regain a measure of composure, exhaling louder than they're inhaling, which isn't the way to do it if you're trying to relax. But try as they might, they can't bring themselves to relax.

Alexis tries to get it in her head that she needs to bathe, but she can't. She can't even bring herself to comb the sweat from her hair so that it lies flat against her face, and Tucker feels like he needs to wipe it from her eyes. But he can't bring himself to touch her, not knowing how to respond to her showing of emotions now. This is the first time that she seems to come undone, and he doesn't know what to do to make it better, to make it all go away. He feels helpless.

"So now we're fugitives," Alexis says, with a hint of humor so that Tucker cannot help but smile. He even manages a rather subdued giggle, and then a laugh. They try to make light of a very serious situation, succeeding very mildly.

"Yeah, it would appear that way," Tucker responds, but he isn't really feeling the humor, and he is uncertain of whether he too will manage to extract a smile from Alexis. But that they're trying is something at least. They look at one another now with a semblance of a smile on their faces, in their eyes, and they say nothing. What can they say that will make this whole situation disappear? They're deep in it now, and they need to think of a way to get out of it.

"I think I need to talk to Chloe," Tucker says, eventually, the beginnings of a plan forming in his head.

. . .

"Do you really think that this is a good idea, Tucker, after what they tried to do to us? Don't you think it's best to leave her out of this for her own safety?" Alexis surprises herself with her concern for Chloe and her well-being. She quizzes herself in her head for the place that this concern might have come from.

"What else are we going to do, and she seems to have the inside scoop on this whole mess. You saw her in that room, heard her on the phone talking to Grant...that...thing...whatever it is, she must know something that can help us." Tucker knows his sister, and he knows her well. She has been given power now, allowed into the inner circle of whatever it is that is going on with the world, and that is something that she will not relinquish easily. But he has to try and convince her to see reason, whatever reason can be seen in this whole horrible mess.

"Let's just call him Grant, for ease of reference," again Alexis tries to spice up the mess they're in with humor. This time it works, and Tucker curls over laughing, at the joke, and at the situation, they find themselves in. In all his years on the force, he never imagined that he would be on this side of the line. It's uncomfortable. And he wishes that he could just cross back over to the other side, the right side. But he knows that he would have to leave Alexis on this uncomfortable side. The choice is an easy one to make, and he decides to stay put and see it through.

But he has to leave her now, at least for a while, to go and see his sister. He would much rather leave her in China-town, amongst people, until he was ready to pick her up again, but she insists on being left in the motel, insisting that she will be fine. After all, if they had spotted them, then they would probably have blown up the motel by now, Alexis reasons.

Reluctantly Tucker leaves her to her thoughts, in the relative safety of the room. They had after all used pseudonyms when they checked it, and they checked in so quickly that the clerk wouldn't have had a chance to get a really good look at them and liken them to the faces now flashing on every television screen in the country at regular intervals. He just seemed too happy for the business, only looking up at Tucker to take the cash from him.

He almost expects Chloe not to be home. He hardly comes to her apartment because she's never there, or at least that's what she tells the doorman to tell him. But she's home, and she will see him. He wonders how much of this has to do with what they know and what he witnessed in the room underneath Alexis's old lab.

"Hey big brother, here to give me a lecture?" she starts, knowing that Tucker has not come to see her just for the sake of. She also knows courtesy of Grant Chambers, that he knows everything about their 'work' downstairs and her involvement in it.

"No, I'm here to ask for your help!" Tucker watches his sister closely now, almost as though he was searching for something that would make her appear less human. I mean, if the aliens could take over Grant Chamber's body so successfully, and those of the world's leaders, what would stop them from simply taking over his sisters too. He sees nothing, recognizing all of her expressions as her own, and her wit and sarcasm also are a dead giveaway.

"What are you looking at Tucker, do you think I'm suddenly going to sprout tentacles and drain you of your blood," Chloe asks, reading her brother's mind. He looks at her like he's just been found out in a lie, and he has to shake himself free of this feeling, letting it fall to the floor with the absurdity of this notion.

"I kind of expected it, I'm not gonna lie," Tucker isn't sure if he is joking, but he says it anyway.

"Oh please Tucker, be serious for once in your life," suddenly her words have an icy edge to them that he can't deny. He doesn't even know where to place himself in this room that feels very much like the first time he is seeing it. He's been to his sister's place once or twice before, but each time it feels like the first time.

He looks around at how impersonal everything is, almost as though his sister refused to get emotionally invested in the space. Or maybe this is his sister's personality, or lack thereof. He can't be sure. He looks around again, for anything that might give away a hint of anything that says 'Chloe' in the room, and again he comes up short. How she can live so detached even from her own reality is beyond him.

"I am serious," he says in his defense, but only after, the accusation of his lack of seriousness almost forgotten. Still, he continues, "You need to talk to your bosses, get them to leave us alone. They blew up the house you know, it's gone, like it never was, almost."

. . .

Chloe doesn't look surprised even though she lets out a loud gasp. Her hand over her mouth is even less convincing. Tucker just observes her little performance, wondering where his sister, the young woman he used to love, has gone. All he sees in front of him now is a cold, hardcore, overly-ambitious charlatan. He shakes his head in disappointment.

"What happened to you," he asks eventually.

"Well, mom and dad died, and that pretty much messed me up. So I fill my days with other pursuits so that I don't have to think about that." Chloe's response is again icy, but Tucker knows that at least this time, she means every word.

"So does that mean that you can just kill all those inno-cent people because you're hurting because you lost out on a happy family? When did you become so selfish?" Tucker really feels sorry for her now.

"I've always been like this; you've just been too preoc-cupied with your idea of how I should be to see me for who I really am." Chloe sounds bitter now, as though she was hurt and angry at the same time. But she quickly recovers from the emotion, and again she is composed and well put-together. Tucker remembers her handbag and his image of his sister changes somewhat. It all seems like an act to him now.

Tucker doesn't respond to this, just letting her have her moment. She obviously needs to indulge in this, whatever this is, and so he lets her. That their parents' death had affected her so badly Tucker didn't know. But now that he does, it still doesn't excuse his sister's behavior, especially what she is doing to people in that room.

"So I take it you won't talk to them then," Tucker asks

finally when he realizes that his sister really isn't the person she once was.

"No Tucker, I'm not going to talk to them. And this is for your own good, trust me." He has no idea what she means until he is taken from the back by many hands. He didn't even realize that they were no longer alone in the apartment. He had no idea when she made the call that brought these men into her apartment, the men who have freed him of his weapon and have his hands behind his back. He looks at his sister, not recognizing her anymore, and not knowing what this means, that she is doing this for 'his own good'. All he knows is that he was completely jaded for a moment in their conversation and now he has been captured.

Tucker struggles momentarily until he is knocked out, an electric shock filtering through his body in waves. By the time he wakes up, he is in an office at the World Government's headquarters, one that only opens from the outside. He knows that screaming for help would be futile, but he takes consolation in the fact that they haven't killed him yet. But he can't help but wonder what they have in store for him.

He checks for his phone, it's obviously gone. What did he expect? He looks around the office, no different from an interrogation room downtown. He wonders how many people have been brought to this very room, against their will, in the last while. He wonders a lot of things, but mostly he worries about Alexis.

Meanwhile back at the motel, Alexis is drifting in and out of sleep. She doesn't want to sleep, growing more and more concerned about Tucker the longer that he's away, but unable to keep her eyes open. The hours slip by, and still no sign of Tucker. She turns on the TV.

In front of her is another flash bulletin. Tucker's picture appears alone in the caption box, and for a moment she thinks that they've given up on her. But she soon realizes why Tucker cuts a solitary figure on the screen, the word 'CAPTURED' splattered across his chest. She can't breathe.

She turns up the volume and for a moment can't make heads or tails of what the reporter is saying. Then the world comes into a strange focus again, and she hears every word, every detail of how Tucker was captured. Somehow she knows that this is a fabrication and that Chloe had something to do with her brother's capture. She really is proving to be some piece of work.

Then her picture is on the screen, the words 'STILL AT LARGE' moving across the screen over her breasts. Again she has to remind herself to breathe, and so she takes a few deep breaths before holding it again, seeming to breathe too loudly so that she can't hear what is being said about her.

It's clear that they're pinning the bombing of her building on her, something about her being a disgruntled employee who weeks earlier had blown up her lab and office. Why would they go through so much trouble to discredit her? She thinks she knows why. Who would listen to, let alone help somebody who was responsible for an explosion that killed 283 people? She didn't even know that so many people lived in her building. And what about Tucker's house, what are they saying about that. A brief mention at the end of the bulletin puts it down to faulty electric systems, probably since the house was so old.

At the end of the bulletin, she turns down the volume but leaves the TV on. She thinks of turning on the lights in the room, and does so, twice, turning them off each time. She shifts between the channels and catches the same news report three times. Each one is the same as the one before, with the common through-line that she would do better to turn herself in.

She curls up on the bed, thinking if perhaps she isn't dreaming. She knows she isn't, more like wishful thinking on her part. She knows that Tucker would never let them know where she is and that the fact they are saying that she should turn herself in means that they have no idea where she is. This fact doesn't comfort her in the least, her mind preoccupied with Tucker, and what they must be doing to him to get her whereabouts out of the murder detective.

One thing is clear though, that she cannot turn herself in. Tucker will just have to be strong, and hold on until she figures out what to do. If the World Government wants a fight, then it's a fight they will get. She will not give them the satisfaction of just handing herself over to them. She knows that Tucker would agree.

She is suddenly very alert. She manages a shower, even though she puts on the same clothes. Even dinner goes down with a burger and fries from the vendor down the road. She needs to keep her strength up or to restore it if the past few days can be blamed for expelling all her energy from her. She has her hoodie pulled far over her head when she makes the purchase, just in case the bohemian chick on the serving end of the counter cared to watch the news at all. Somehow she doubts it.

So they're summoning her to headquarters. This thought mulls around in her head, and she plays out what might happen if she indeed just rocked up there and presented herself to 'them'. She plays out several scenarios in her head, none of them ending very well, for her, or Tucker. She realizes what she needs to do, but it won't be easy. She calls a cab, and just in time remembers the pseudonym she used to check in to the motel.

She has the cabby drive around for a while as she tinkers away at her computer. She is no computer geek, but getting information from the Internet is pretty standard stuff, amateurish even. She checks out some underground sites and pulls some names, mostly from urban legend, but she has to cover all her bases. After about two hours she has a couple of addresses and she randomly selects one, handing it to the cab driver.

"Are you sure?" he asks her, keeping his eyes on the road.

"Yes, I'm sure," is Alexis's response, although she really isn't. She isn't sure of anything anymore except the fact that she needs to get Tucker out of the World Government headquarters, away from the aliens, and away from that room, with its teleporting chambers.

She moves around the club, the first address on the list, feeling horribly underdressed; or overdressed, depending on who you were looking at. After she makes a few inquiries it's clear that she is on the right track. She is directed to someone who directs her to someone else, and then she is standing in front of the person she was looking for.

Soon she is gathering quite an army of underground types, anybody that will listen to her story of alien invasions and rebellion. She speaks to some people, and midway during the conversation suddenly stops, realizing that they're looking at her like she's mad. Others are really enthusiastic about her cause, having caught their pictures on the news and that, coupled with Alexis's cell phone images, is too exciting a deal to pass up.

One thing is clear though, that most people are prepared to do what needs to be done to preserve our way of life. And not the way of life that the aliens have brought us, but true humanity. She works through her list, gathering people who will stand with her as she goes.

It's still unclear to her what her plan is when they arrive at the World Government, but she is sure that by the time she has worked through her list, she will have some idea of what to do. She keeps at it for most of the night, and by the first light of dawn, she is quite tired but strangely alert. She puts this down to adrenalin. There are a few more names on the list, but she isn't sure if daytime is a good time to search for these people. She has to trust herself though, now more than she ever has in her life.

CHAPTER 11

ALEXIS DOESN'T KNOW who to trust really, but she has no choice but to try. And she knows that every person she tells puts Tucker's life in more danger. Who knows what they are doing to him right now, or if he is even still on the planet.

But human beings are a strange bunch. Given a common cause, they will rally behind each other for the achievement of that purpose; and what better purpose to be united under? She feels the pressure of time though now, knowing that it takes just minutes for them to teleport a human being to god-knows-where. And if that is Tucker's fate, then she really needs to get to him quickly.

They move through the sewer system that runs under the city, but can't reach the World Government headquarters this way. The sewer system under the building is protected by impenetrable grids, metal grills that they just can't get through. This is understandable, given what is going on in the real basement of the building. They will have to go in the front door.

But how, with seven security checkpoints before you even enter the building. Alexis is suddenly overwhelmed by the task at hand, not sure how to proceed, or if they even can. She sits under an open manhole and looks up to catch the night sky. She wonders, if alien life is possible just beyond the stars, is it not also possible that God exists beyond that? She needs something to believe in, and quickly, Tucker not having much time left, she thinks.

She looks back, and around her. She has managed to gather quite an army. But they will be no match for the World Government's guards, especially if they come at them with all they've got. What to do?

Then she remembers the old war museum. It has working replicas of every weapon and tank ever made. And it's not too far from the World Government's headquarters, so they won't see them coming. If they can just get past the museum's guards then they will be home, and hopefully, have Tucker with them.

They see one guard, smoking on the outside of the building. But he is definitely not the only one. Alexis can't even make herself look any sort of sexy to distract him, she is just a mess. So she uses her messiness and heads straight up to the guard. "Help, help me!" she says, pulling on her skirt as though she was the victim of some horrible violation. The guard puts out his cigarette and walks over to her, not sure if he should touch her, not sure what to do. He's stunned silent, never having been confronted with such a scenario in all his years as a security guard.

With his gaze on Alexis, and his arms helplessly outstretched, they see a gap, and C-lo, a young member of Alexis's army comes up to him and puts an arm around his throat. The guard loses consciousness to the sound of Alexis saying 'I'm sorry, I'm sorry!'

Once they're inside the building they know that they've probably been seen on the CCTV cameras, and so they need to move quickly. They have to be brazen in their approach, quickly in, taking what they want, and getting out. The police are probably already on their way. Two more security guards make a feeble attempt to stop them, but they too are rendered unconscious by a similar chokehold.

Finally, they are in the Hall of Memories, where Alexis remembered seeing three large tanks the first time she was here. To her delight, the exhibit hasn't changed much, and right in front of them, are three large war tanks. Now they just need to get them to work.

A group goes off to see what else they can find. And what they come back with is priceless, headgear, with the ability to connect via satellite to every TV screen in the world. They take these communication tools and test them. They work!

Soon enough the tanks hum to life and then growl a deep growl from being used once a year at the exhibition. Now to get them out of here, and there is no neat and tidy way to do this.

. . .

There are people inside the tanks and on them. Bodies hang precariously from anything that they can grip on. It's show-time, and time is something they will not have a lot of. Alex-is's thoughts shift between Tucker and how the hell they're going to get out of here without being shot at.

C-lo is proving to be quite handy. Armed with nothing but Alexis's laptop, he manages to intercept the world's broadcast satellite. Screens all over the world go fuzzy, and then snowy. He knows that he is in. He redirects them to the coms, creating one solid frequency on which images and audio can be transmitted right from the headgear to living rooms all over the world. He looks at Alexis, and her image instantly fills the screens across the globe.

They are in the foyer to the museum, the front door right in front of them. Without even thinking, they burst through the massive structures, sending glass and wood everywhere. Blue lights can be made out in the distance. They have a company.

Alexis manages to get on top of the tank that she's in, and hopes for the best. She will have to get the police to give them a gap. They just need to get to the World Government and stream the images of the extra-terrestrials all over the place, so that the world will know what is going on.

The tanks move slowly to the gate, and once they get there, they are surrounded by the first battalion of blue lights. Police officers quickly get out of their cars and take aim. It's now or never.

. . .

"Wait, wait, don't shoot!" she screams.

"Get out of the tanks," a police officer says through a bullhorn.

"Wait!" she begs, and the cops don't know what to make of this. They thought that the commotion was caused by riotous teenagers, but Alexis is an adult. They hold their fire, fingers on the triggers. Alexis goes on to explain what is happening.

The whole world sits up and takes note. Images of the cops with their guns pointed at Alexis and her companions flash across their screens so that the people sitting in front of their TVs think that they're watching a science fiction movie. But this is no movie. Everything that they are seeing is happening right now, in real time, and a nervous tension settles across the globe.

Everyone thinks that the world has been taken over by terrorists so that the nervous tension soon becomes anxiety. Alexis realizes that this looks bad and that everyone is probably rooting for the trigger-happy cops. She thinks quickly, going into combat mode, which is strange for her since she's never been in combat.

"I can prove that everything that I'm saying is the truth. But you will have to trust me. Let us pass, and soon you will all know the truth." She speaks to the cops, begging them, but knowing that what she is saying is carrying very little weight, and they are just aiming for a clear shot of her. She thinks of Tucker, and hopes that he has some friends on the force left, people that will trust that he wouldn't get involved with terrorist activity, and people that she hopes will give her a chance to prove that she hasn't completely lost her mind. Then she remembers her cell phone. The battery is incredibly low, but she hands it down to C-lo anyway. "The pictures," she screams at him, almost too loud. He is already on it. Before long the pictures Alexis took in that room are streamed live across the world, and the police check the monitors that come standard with every cop car. Some of them are more shocked then others, some think that this is just all an elaborate hoax. But there are enough cops surrounding them who think that maybe, just maybe Alexis hasn't completely lost her mind.

The sight of these massive tanks causes quite a stir on the roads. People stop and stare, cars stopping, one after the other, bumper to bumper, to create the space needed by these monstrosities to move. Still, it's a very tight squeeze.

Alexis has one goal in mind, now that the cops have let them through, and that is getting to the World Government headquarters in time to save Tucker. It will be very premature of them to do anything to him, without at least using him as collateral to get her there, she reasons. But reason seems to have gone out the window now, and the world's leaders seem to have lost their mind. Or at least their bodies.

As the World Government headquarters comes into focus Alexis has a sharp pain in her side. It's probably been there for a while, but with all the adrenalin running through her, she probably never noticed it. Or perhaps it's the sheer excitement of everything, now that they are coming upon their destination. What will it all mean for the rest of the world, the world that she has come to know, when this secret is out?

They approach the gate, and the first security check-point comes into view. But they will need collateral of their own, if they are to have any hope of successfully storming the building. Alexis turns to C-lo who is now her right hand, and asks him if he can use the laptop to find an address.

"Of course, I can, whose address do you need?" is the enthusiastic response. Alexis wished that this kid was her assistant back in the days when she still had a lab and a job. They turn a sharp left just as they come upon the front gate to the World Government. A small detour is necessary.

They come up to Chloe's apartment building. It's the middle of the night, but everyone is already peeping out of their windows to see the commotion on the street. The brave are out in the streets, gawking at the huge tanks escorted by the police. People start to pass around their own interpretations of what is going on. They're all wrong of course, but with so much excitement in the streets who cares.

Alexis, C-lo, and two meaty beefcakes called T-Rex and Samson storm the building. They march straight past the security guard and enter the elevator. Nobody even tries to stop them. They go outside instead to look at the tanks, symbols of a war a long time ago. They assume that it is the army and therefore they stay out of their way.

"What the..." Chloe is throwing on a nightgown in her bedroom when Alexis and her crew enter.

"Shut up. Where do you keep your access cards?" Alexis has had enough. She turns her handbag out, the contents going all over the place.

"My what? Alexis?" Chloe finally registers who it is and

looks around the room at the muscle. She looks to where her phone is ringing on the side table.

"Don't even think about it. Let's go," Alexis says, the muscle grabbing Chloe as Alexis takes the access cards off the floor. They march right out of the building with little resistance from anybody, not even Chloe, who seems more concerned with her nightgown than anything else.

They get her in the tank and once again they're headed for the World Government. They've completely forgotten about the coms on their heads now and just go through the motions of what needs to be done. It makes for riveting viewing through, and even in the parts of the world where people are supposed to be sleeping, they now sit up in front of the TV, anxious to know what will happen next.

They get to the World Government headquarters and don't even wait for a second before storming the facility. One, two, three security checkpoints cleared, completely destroyed, the guards that took refuge behind the guard-houses now cowering behind the rubble. Four, five, six, and then seven security checkpoints cleared, and then they are on the outside of the building. By now the guards are pulling themselves together, on their radios, letting their colleagues inside know what's up.

Alexis looks at Chloe, and she knows what she has to do. Resistance now would be futile. She can only hope that the guards inside will be more diligent than the ones on the outside of the building. She places her finger on the scanner, and then looks directly at the retinal scanner. The door slides open, and immediately the foyer to the headquarters fills with vigilantes. Alexis knows exactly where she needs to get to first, and with Chloe and her access cards, they make for the staircase.

The soldiers in the foyer look confused for a second, and then they pull their weapons. Alexis just has to hope that Chloe is collateral enough for them not to fire. No gunshots are heard, and she pulls Chloe towards the staircase. She looks at her fellow vigilantes, and they know that they need to spread out. But they are only armed with stun guns, and comparing these to the weapons that are now facing them, it's like chalk and cheese, but they have to rely on the fact that even the screens in the World Government are now showing images from their headgear.

And this is what protects them. The fact that the whole world is watching stands them in good stead, that they can take the staircase and go up the various floors, looking for Tucker. Alexis speaks directly into her communication device's mouthpiece and lets the whole world know that they've come to rescue Tucker, but first she has something to show everyone.

Chloe looks at her with a 'do you know what you're doing' look. She doesn't, but it's too late to turn back now. "Just get on with it," she orders, handing Chloe her access cards. Chloe has no choice but to let her and her accomplices into the 'lab' with its rows and rows of extra-terrestrials.

Alexis walks into the room, adjusting her headgear unnecessarily so that the rows and rows come into view. It takes a moment, but soon the scene comes into focus, and everybody watching the scene sits on the edge of their seats, or stands. They adjust their heads, not sure what they are looking at for a while, but then it becomes clear. Alexis walks among the rows slowly.

The others too walk slowly, streaming their visuals to the rest of the world. Chloe stands back, unable to move, not believing that Alexis has been so brazen. She watches as Alexis and her partners move through the lab, streaming the images live. How can this be happening she wonders, as she starts pacing in the center courtyard?

The whole world now sits up and takes note; clearly, they're not being punked. This is obviously not a joke, and so the anxiety is now collective. Everybody wants to start something, preparing for something, but what. How will they escape from these aliens, and where will they escape to?

They are sitting on the edge of their seats, watching the aliens that seem to be sleeping, anticipating that they will wake up any moment. Alexis too is fearful that these will rise any time, but at least the whole world will have seen them. And this awareness will be all she hopes necessary to send these beings packing.

As she completes what she thinks will be sufficient shooting of the aliens the world's leaders are going insane. They have their own communication going with Grant Chambers, demanding to know how this could have happened on his watch. They wish, particularly China, that another alien, one more advanced, more civilized, had been assigned the task of taking over the Chambers' body.

"I've got this under control," is all Grant can manage,

although it is clear to all the leaders now watching the dirty laundry being aired in public that this isn't the case. Grant will have to sort this out, and quickly, or else earth and all its inhabitants are doomed. Grant is caught up in a conundrum, saving this planet with its ready source of human capital, or destroying the whole lot.

He searches all his brains; he has three, for a solution to the current predicament, but can come up with nothing. Meanwhile, the aliens inhabiting the world leaders are becoming increasingly impatient with him. In fact, they've become quite restless, realizing that they have sent 3000 of their best to this planet to oversee things, never once thinking that the humans on earth would ever wise up to the antics, and certainly not anticipating a revolution of this magnitude. They concur that they have all grossly misjudged Alexis's intellect, and the tenacity of human beings, once threatened.

Alexis has shown the world enough for her to think that anybody who didn't believe her now was either incredibly stupid or suffering from the worst form of denial. She gathers her troops, and after one more shot of the room in its entirety, she leaves, with her army in tow. They head for the staircase, and proceed up, past the blown-up lab and office. They try Chloe's cards on the door that they encounter, and remarkably, the fourth card that they try gets them through it. She can't help but be hurt at how much the World Government trusted Chloe with these all-access passes, and how quickly. But she will have time to wallow in her resentment later, right now, they need to find Tucker.

They move swiftly through the long corridors, C-lo checking periodically that they still have an established connection with the satellites that are providing them with the leverage they need to move through the building without being shot.

But all of them, especially Alexis, just waits for the first shot that is going to be fired, resulting in more shots, and all of them dying in the hands of the World Government; after all, what does the World Government, or rather, what do these aliens have to lose?

Still, she steels herself against this thought, overriding her own need for survival with Tucker's. How his sister could of betrayed him like that is still a mystery to Alexis, one that she knows she will never solve, judging by the look in Chloe's eyes. She seems absent, almost as though she was not even present here anymore. She is probably dealing with the loss of power once again to her arch-nemesis in the only way she knows how, by retracting into her own head, where everything makes sense, at least to her.

Doors fling open, mostly office doors that are void of the elaborate entry mechanism of some of the other doors. Predictably they find these empty, most of them looking like they haven't been used in a very long time. Just how long have these aliens been here, and who was responsible for the calendar that foresaw all this, Alexis wonders. Surely the Mayans could not have been so forward-thinking, despite the calendars having been found amongst their relics.

As Alexis and her followers make their way up through

the various floors Tucker is unaware of the commotion. He looks around the room that he is in, trying to find a way out. But the room is very high up, probably thirty stories high, and so escaping through the window is impossible, which explains the lack of burglar bars on them. Still, he lifts his chair and tries to smash it through the glass. But the chair simply bounces back and lands on its side on the floor. He will not be getting out that way.

He looks at the door for a long time, almost willing it to open. It doesn't, obviously, and the frustration starts to get to him until he reminds himself to breathe. He has been in stickier situations before, although at the moment it is difficult for him to remember even one. In fact, he searches his head for anything that he can use as a reference for the situation he currently finds himself in, and comes up with nothing.

But Alexis is getting closer and closer to where he is being held. She knows this because security seems to get tighter the higher up she goes. She catches the sun rising out of the windows of one of the empty rooms, and realizes that they've been in the building for a very long time. But she commits to turning the building inside out before she will give up on finding Tucker.

Still, the security gets tighter, but as soon as the guards realize that they are being filmed, they seem to forget their guns, at least for the moment. Nobody even tries to stop Alexis and her bandits as they turn the building out in their search. Alexis gets the feeling that she is walking closer and closer to an ambush, and so she checks with her followers if any of them want to turn back. Unanimously they agree that since they've come so far already, they may as well see it through to the end, whatever the end means for them in the current circumstance.

They are greeted with locked doors on the twenty-eighth floor, and entry seems impossible. Even Chloe's access cards will not get them into the row of locked doors. Chloe mumbles something about not having clearance at this level, and Alexis has no choice but to believe her. They have to think of another way around this obstacle.

When it's clear that there is no way inside these doors C-lo hands Alexis the computer and disappears down the hall and into the door that leads to the staircase they've just come through. He seems to be gone forever, and Alexis checks with the others if she shouldn't perhaps go and try and find them. They decide to give them ten more minutes before doing anything. She looks at Chloe, still absent in her eyes despite her body being here with them. She has a million questions for the researcher, but she decides not to ask a single one. They wait, nervously, leaning against the wall as if this might make them invisible should anyone appear through the elevator doors at the end of the corridor. But nobody appears, and soon enough C-lo and the men he took with him reappear through the staircase door.

"These might come in handy," he says, holding up two guns. The men he is with are also armed suddenly. Alexis doesn't even want to know how they got these guns, probably something to do with the chokehold he is so skilled at. It takes to shots to shoot through the locks on the first door, but they find the office empty. They shoot through the mechanisms on every door in the long corridor, but find every single office empty, but with definite signs of life.

When they fire the first shots through the first door on the thirtieth floor Tucker thinks he is imagining things. But then the sound gets closer, and he knows that he isn't hearing things. Those are definitely gunshots.

But what could it mean, Tucker wonders, looking around the sparsely furnished room for a place to hide. He sees nothing that could form a barrier between him and the gunshots that are definitely coming closer. What is going on? He stands up from the chair that he has restored to the position it was intended to be in, and moves to the corner of the room, a reflex. But he knows that there is no escape from the gunfire coming his way.

Everyone watches with bated breath as they fire round after round into the doors, which give way easily under the power of the firearms. The guards were definitely not trained to fire warning shots, Alexis thinks, as they approach the office that Tucker is being held prisoner in.

The world watches, all of them rooting for Tucker's rescue now. Alexis never neglects her world audience, giving them a blow-by-blow account of what they are doing. Most of the world frowns each time Chloe comes into shot, and they all hope without saying it that Alexis would just take a weapon and put a bullet in her head. But Alexis isn't cut from that cloth, and the thought doesn't even cross her mind.

. . .

They fire one shot, then another, into the office door where Tucker is, almost expecting that this one too will be empty. As the door comes off its hinges and swings into the room C-lo is the first to enter, with the laptop. He cast a casual glance from corner to corner, missing Tucker for the first time with his eyes. But the com on his head captures him in view so that the whole world breathes a collective sigh of relief.

'There, there he is,' can be heard from almost everyone watching, almost as though the guy with the laptop can hear them. And then he sees him, so that he wants to put the laptop down, but instead he checks that the visual on Tucker is good. He looks back out of the room at Alexis and smiles broadly. She knows that this could mean just one thing, and she pushes her way into the room.

She stands back for a moment in disbelief, Tucker already walking towards her. He throws his arms around her, and then plants a very passionate kiss on her lips, out of focus for the world, but they know what is going on. Wolf whistles sound from every living room across the globe. The couple kisses for an eternity until Tucker sees his sister just looking at them.

He pulls away from Alexis for a minute and just stares at his sister, not knowing what he should say to her. He really has no words for her and her traitorous ways. So he just shakes his head, and resumes his position on Alexis's mouth, kissing her with more passion now, forgetting that they have an audience, and forgetting that they have the small matter of getting the hell out of there to contend with.

When they finally stop kissing they realize a few truths about their position. They are thirty stories up, and they've probably pissed off every alien on the planet. The aliens must be making plans for their demise, or the demise of the whole planet, as they speak. Alexis wonders how many of the natural disasters that have befallen humanity over the last couple of millennia have actually been 'natural'. Not many, she thinks to herself but doesn't say it out loud so as not to scare anyone.

But now the whole world knows what is going on, and what has probably been going on for a while. What they will do with what they know remains to be seen, but it is clear that they will not be able to battle the aliens with their primitive weapons. The whole world seems destined to become a penal colony, one where humans are bred for the sole purpose of servicing the aliens' needs on their native planets.

"So what are we gonna do now," she asks Tucker, handing the reigns over to him once he has sufficiently recovered.

"Well, since we're already here, I think we need to go up and see a certain 'Mr. Chambers' don't you," he responds while looking at his sister. Her countenance is somewhat fallen, as she realizes that everything she thought she had gained is slowly slipping from her grasp. Chloe looks away, unable to look her brother in the eye now, finally realizing the true meaning of everything that she has done here.

Tucker takes Alexis by the hand and grabs one of the guns that C-lo wields effortlessly even with the laptop in his hands. He seems relieved to be free of the piece so that he can focus his energies on the true skill he possesses.

They walk towards the elevators now, just to try Chloe's fingerprint and retinal scan, almost certain that they will work. They don't, so they quickly make for the staircase, knowing that Grant Chambers will be in the penthouse, trapped, like the alien that he is, in its icy grip, unable to leave.

They take the stairs up to the last door that leads out into a long corridor that has just one elevator at the end of it. The door opens onto this corridor, and not directly into the presidential suite as they had hoped. The president obviously has another, more elaborate means of escaping in the event of a fire, or any other disaster that might befall him. And from what they now know, many things could befall the alien that has taken over the body of the frazzled Grant Chambers.

They walk up to the elevator and give it all the firepower they have between them, but nothing. The door doesn't budge, and shows no signs of opening. Then C-lo comes to the rescue, understanding the system that keeps the doors locked. He rips the console from the wall, and after a moment of fiddling with the wires that he finds underneath it, the doors to the lift slide open.

Inside the lift are two more elevator doors, one to the left, and one to the right. They are in familiar territory now, Tucker and Alexis, knowing that the one on the right leads into the office, the one on the left, into the boardroom. They go for the office elevator first.

After a moment, the doors slide open, leaving the console dangling on the outside of the doors. Tucker is the first to enter, holding Alexis close, but behind him. Chloe is with another beefcake whose name slips everybody's mind. But they're glad to have this anonymous force containing the hurricane that is Chloe.

Tucker's eyes dart from corner to corner in the large room, and he sees nothing. He looks over to the scotch, with its signature glasses next to the bottle, and immediately wants a swig from the bottle. But now is not the time for such indulgences. Alexis too is searching the space for Grant Chambers. But he is not here.

Everyone except Tucker, Chloe, and Alexis looks around the space with awe, feeling the icy chill creep up and down their spines like a million spiders. They have one question on their minds, a question that they answer for themselves soon enough. This is no longer the president's office. It is a lair, an alien lair, but the alien that they are all looking for is not here.

After everyone has had their fill of the room they all look around for the door leading directly to the boardroom, following Tucker's eyes. They look at the elaborate door and wonder if they should go through it now, suddenly feeling like they've reached their final destination. Tucker makes the decision for all of them, and he walks towards the doors, reaching for the handle long before he arrives at the door.

. . .

He tries it and finds it locked. Naturally! He looks over at C-lo, who looks confused for a second since this door isn't like the elevators. It doesn't look like it has an elaborate system of entry. But Tucker knows better, so does Alexis.

They show C-lo the elaborate access point, carefully hidden under even more elaborate woodwork. He lights up at the sight, enjoying any and every technological challenge. But this one is indeed more advanced than the previous ones he worked on, and so it takes him longer to get through.

Tucker becomes increasingly impatient, and he points his gun at the complicated mechanism. But C-lo is quick to ask him for a little more time, assuring him that there is yet to be designed a lock that he cannot crack. He steps back and lets the young man work, but his finger remains ready on the trigger.

Inside the boardroom, red lights are flashing everywhere. It's not that there is danger outside the door that could harm the president mind you, it's the world's leaders, anxious to speak with Grant Chambers. He looks at the button that will bring them all into view, but he doesn't press it, still uncertain of what he will say to them, or of what they have to say to him.

Grant paces the length of the room, moving behind the seats, looking up at the blank screens. He tries to remember the day they hired Alexis, thinking that she would just come into the World Government and 'do her job'. He realizes that they were very wrong about her. And this is the price that they have to pay for underestimating a human being the way they have.

Humans were much easier to manipulate in times gone by. They were primitive, and as long as they were fed, they were happy. It was so easy to convince them that human sacrifice was essential to the survival of the species. They had many more sacrifices back then. But times had indeed changed, and this was a testament to just how big a change had happened.

He is again in front of the button, anxiety seeping through his veins like heroin. It's not a pleasant rush. Grant puts his finger on the button but he doesn't press it. He lifts it off, with great difficulty, knowing that he has to give an account for everything that has gone down, everything that is still going down at the World Government's headquarters.

Searching his head for a plan that he can present to the world's leaders, or rather to the aliens that inhabit their bodies, he comes up short, finding himself wanting. He wishes that he could just go downstairs and climb into one of the chambers and be teleported home. But he knows that this is not possible, not now.

Finally, he just lets his finger fall on the button. It takes a while for the world's leaders to come into view with the satellite scrambled by C-lo's efforts. But eventually, they do, and there is not a happy face in the room, except for Russia, who doesn't seem to understand the difference between a smile and a frown.

Nobody says anything for a while, and it is Grant who now looks like the naughty schoolboy outside the principal's office. He looks down, unable to face any of the aliens who had wanted this assignment but lost out to him in a vote.

The 'I told you so' looks from all of them is just too much for him to bear. But they all look at him, and then from one to the other, wondering who will go first. There is no hierarchy here, just a group of aliens who decided that earth was as good a place as any to extract a suitable workforce from.

CHAPTER 12

C-LO IS STILL BATTLING with the mechanism on the outside of the room, while inside Grant is battling with the world's leaders. Brazil has finally broken the silence, saying what is on everyone's mind. He looks more than a little pissed off.

"So, well done Grant, you really messed this up!" His use of the word 'grant' is somewhat sarcastic so that Australia smirks.

"But how could I have foreseen this, none of us could have anticipated this." Grant is defensive, trying to shift the blame proportionately to all of them, not succeeding.

"But you're the president of the world, you should have seen this coming," Brazil continues, not letting up, and definitely digging his heels in.

"None of us saw this coming, how was I supposed to know that the girl was so bright?" Grant continues on his defensive streak.

"Because she is not a girl Grant, she is a very intuitive

young woman. Did you learn nothing in all the preparations we did with you for this mission?" All Brazil needed to say is 'I told you so', but he is enjoying this too much.

"Okay I messed up, but what are we going to do about this now?" Grant finally admits defeat, and he admits in one sentence that he doesn't know what to do about this, about the humans on the other side of the door, about the fact that the whole world knows now that they are here, and what they are doing.

"We, Mr. Chambers?" Brazil is determined to put it all on Grant. He really doesn't see how any of them can be blamed for this.

"Yes we, dammit, we!" Grant is angry now at the insinuation that this is all his fault. It really is.

The rest of the 'world's leaders' proceed to have a heated conversation that has nothing to do with Grant Chambers. They seem to have already dismissed him as a leader, each one secretly hating all the power they gave to this idiot. Grant looks very uncomfortable now, knowing that this will probably not end well for him.

He can just watch as they plan an exit strategy, no talk of simply blowing the whole planet up and starting again. What would the point be, after all? Human beings are not a threat to them, or at least they weren't a threat until they started harvesting them. It really all is a monumental mess.

Grant thinks to put forth a few suggestions but decides against it. Nobody is even addressing him now, and he hates it. He really enjoyed being the president of this little planet, regardless of how uncomfortable it was for him physically.

They had voted, and he had won, almost as though he had won a legitimate election. But now that power has slipped from his grasp completely. He just stands to the side quietly and lets them talk over the situation.

Just then the door separating them from the humans slides open, and in walk the humans, Alexis and Tucker leading. Chloe cannot look at Grant Chambers now, feeling the weight of the world on her delicate little shoulders. She thinks that it is all her fault and that they will find a way to blame her. She can only imagine what punishment will be in store for her if this goes the aliens' way.

Alexis looks around at the screens, the world's leaders locked in conversation so that they don't see them come in at first. Even Grant is oblivious to the intrusion for a while, the door sliding open silently, and his head buzzing with the noise of his own demise. He is sure that he will be killed for this.

They go undetected in the room just long enough for the world leaders to incriminate themselves, giving up that they are not of this world. People all over the globe are now no longer anxious, they are angry. How could they have been fooled for so long, and what has happened to their real leaders?

The fact that the world leaders haven't appeared in public should have been the first sign that something was up. But who knows about the eccentricities of politicians these days. So they ignored the first sign. There have been other things too, the earth's people think, but only now, in the current context, does it all make sense.

. . .

But then Grant looks up, the light streaming in from the open door finally catching his attention. He wants to tell the world leaders to shut up, but it's too late. He looks at Chloe, who doesn't look at him. He thinks back to the original interviews, and wonders if perhaps she wouldn't have been better suited for Alexis's job from the very beginning. But it is too late for such wonderings.

Then China spots Alexis, in the room, amongst them. He sees her before he sees anybody else. But soon enough all the rebels have come into view, and the world government knows that the jig is up. Again a deathly silence fills the room, tangible almost in its thickness. The world leaders look at one another, not sure this time who will break the silence.

They clear their throats over and over again. Grant Chambers seems to cower into a corner, although he is trying to stand up as straight as the body he is inhabiting will allow. But it's a futile act, everyone in the room knowing now what they are, and what they have done here.

"You should not have come here," Alexis is the first to speak.

"And why not my dear? You were doing a pretty good job of messing things up, so we just thought we would capitalize on your stupidity." Grant is almost returning to his old self, wanting to prove to the world leaders that he has this under control, that he can handle these humans.

"Oh shut up Grant, she's right. We should not have come here. The question is, now, now that we are here, what are we going to do about it?" China has all but taken over the dialogue.

"You need to leave, now. And never come back. Leave us to mess things up, we will fix it, on our own, without interference from anyone, or anything!" The conversation is between China and Alexis now, the others using their coms to catch every detail of the world leaders. But nothing except for what they say gives them away as aliens. It is really quite remarkable.

"We could do that I suppose, but where in the world will we get such a ready supply of livestock, so easily adaptable, to do the laborious tasks of building our planets?" China's reference to human beings as livestock pisses Alexis off so that she grabs the gun from Tucker and shoots at the screen, which fuzzes for a moment and then goes blank. Communication with China was lost.

"We are not livestock, we are human beings!" Alexis is getting more and more angry and she points the guns at the various screens in the room, daring them to make another such reference.

Russia takes over the conversation, realizing that more tact will be needed in dealing with these humans. He chooses his words very carefully, not wanting to go the same way as China, losing out on the conversation that is being had here.

"Alexis, you are of course right, we should not have come here in the first place, but you must understand how the universe works," he starts, each word coming out with great pain, knowing that the wrong word will see his screenshot at and him out of the loop with regards to the conversation that is going on.

"And just how does the universe work, enlighten us, please!" Alexis is trying hard not to shout, but she is practically screaming at the screen. She can't help herself, hating that these things came here to tell them how it was going to be, and then proceeded to do whatever they liked on our planet.

"I will, in a moment, but don't you think this is a conversation that we should be having privately?" He gestures to the coms so that Alexis knows that he wants them to turn them off.

"Not a chance," she responds. "So that you can just kill us here and put it off to some or other rebellion, only for you to return to harvesting us! I think not!" Her use of the word 'harvesting sets her back somewhat, and she realizes that she too is starting to think of human beings as anything but.

"And why would we do that? You have done sufficient damage to our operations here so that we have one of two choices now, but really, Alexis, is it necessary to put the whole world in a state of panic, having them privy to every detail of this conversation?"

She realizes that what he has to say to her is probably best said without the world as an audience. Besides, they have achieved what they set out to achieve, and the whole world knows now that the world has been run by aliens. Everyone is fully aware of what is going on, and they can make up their own minds what to do about it.

She looks at the others, who look at her, 'are you sure'

written all over their faces. "I'm sure," she says, and the coms are cut. But the tension in the room is thick now, and the tension and anxiety in living rooms across the globe is tangible almost. What will become of their heroes now, everyone wonders?

People all over the world watch blank screens for a while, and then they realize that they are not going to come back on. They gather in meeting places, restaurants, community halls, anywhere where there is sufficient space to house them. They need to come up with a plan and fast.

New York is the epicenter of this invasion, and New Yorkers are not about to take it lying down. They gather all the ammunition that they can get their hands on, everyone who is of arms-bearing age, and they have meetings to decide what to do next. Although it's clear what needs to be done, they want it to be put to a vote, the decision has to come from the majority.

Aliens came to this planet because we couldn't work together, because we all pulled our own ways despite having a common purpose. Well, the humans were about to show them just how together we can be. After a short briefing, it is unanimous, and the army of civilian soldiers heads for the World Government headquarters, unsure of what they will do when they get there, but not caring too much about that right now.

Meanwhile back at headquarters, the aliens try to strike up a deal with Alexis, one that is along the lines of the one that they struck with the world leaders before they took over their bodies.

.   .   .

"You see, we could do each other a favor of sorts, you giving us your unsavory types, and thereby ridding your planet of scum," Russia is losing his tact.

"We have problems, yes, but we would like the opportunity to fix our own problems thank you very much!" Alexis speaks with great authority for every human being on the planet, even the unsavory ones.

"The way I see it, you have one of two choices, you can either willingly give us the capital we need, and go about your business without any real interference from us, or we can simple take what we want!" Russia is no longer begging, finding it to be beneath him to negotiate with a human being for so long. And this negotiation has gone on long enough.

"You should really have stuck to cloning us because we would rather rip out our wombs before we produce a work-force for you!" Alexis is very passionate now about what she is saying, and she is certain that the world's women would feel the same way. "So, the way I see it, you can take what you want, but this will be the last shipment of human beings, we will not keep on producing children just for you to take them as slaves. Yes, we will die out, and yes it will be the end of humanity, but it will be a far nobler death than to die as a slave on some godforsaken planet." She has said all she is going to say on this matter.

Alexis looks around at her fellow humans for agreement, and they all agree with her. Enough is enough, and they have had enough of this. C-lo fires a single shot at the screen with Russia on it, "Bingo!" he yells.

They look at Grant Chambers, wanting to kill him but not sure if the real Grant Chambers is not still in there somewhere. They restrain themselves, and just tie him to a chair. They wonder what to do with Chloe, but the muscle she is with seems comfortable enough with her and so they leave them be. Tucker wouldn't be able to hurt his sister anyway, no matter what she did to him. He resolves in his head and heart immediately to forgive her and to move on with what little life he might have left. After all, nobody really knows what the aliens are going to do.

They shoot out the remaining screens so that the world's leaders have no idea what is going on at headquarters anymore. The world leaders go insane, trying in vain to re-establish a connection, but nothing. Brazil's screen actually falls to the floor, and crashes face down on the marble. It splinters into a million pieces.

The rebels wonder what to do next, and after the screens have all been shot out they are suddenly quiet, not sure of the next move. Even Tucker is at a loss, and he has been designated their leader.

"Right, we might as well go out in flames!" he says finally, and everyone looks at him confused. "It's just an expression, don't worry, I'm not about to blow any of you up!" He almost laughs at the idea.

But somebody isn't laughing. C-lo has an idea. He takes the laptop and puts it on the table, working frantically on it so that the others know not to disturb him. Some people go over to Grant Chambers, looking for evidence of an extraterrestrial, finding none. They prod and prick him, but he doesn't respond, having resigned himself to whatever fate has in store for him.

"Yes," C-lo exclaims so that Alexis and Tucker are again looking over his shoulder.

"What is it," Alexis asks, not sure what all the codes filtering up on the screen in front of her means. But just then the machine starts to beep. Battery low! They look around the room for somewhere to plug it into, and they see nothing. Then Alexis remembers the times she did presentations for the world leaders and takes C-lo and the machine to the end of the table. There is a cable underneath it that fits the slot perfectly.

"That was close," C-lo says before he enters into an elaborate explanation of what he has just done.

"In English dude, please," everyone seems to say at once.

"Okay, okay, I'm in the World Government's security mainframe. They have a self-destruct mechanism in place in case of terror attacks, so that valuable information doesn't fall into enemy hands. In short, if you want to, we can blow this whole building to smithereens!" He sounds very pleased with himself.

"Then that's exactly what we will do!" Tucker remembers his family home, leveled to the ground. This is the perfect revenge. But first they need to get all the information that will help them pick up the pieces after the building is no more.

He gives everybody the instruction to get all the computer hard drives in the building since C-lo won't have the time to download everything. With no time to waste, they get to work, going through the offices that are now thankfully opened, thanks to their shooting spree earlier.

Alexis and Tucker take C-lo with them, once the computer that he is working on has juiced up sufficiently. They also power up their coms again, so that everyone across the world is once again privy to the goings on inside the building. This is their only leverage. It is the only thing that will keep them from being shot.

They make quick work of it, while Alexis and Tucker make their way down the many stairs that will get them to the basement of the building. Alexis just needs one last look at the aliens housed there, before they send them all to hell, or wherever it is that aliens go when they die.

The whole world watches now as the World Government is turned in on itself. Mostly they watch Grant Chambers, who seems to be getting less and less comfortable outside of his icy tower. They can only hope that the real Chambers is still somewhere inside his own body.

He is because by the time they reach the twentieth floor Grant suddenly stops, and breaks free from the two men holding him. He puts a hand over each ear, as though he was hearing a piercing noise that nobody else can hear. Then he drops to his knees, heaving loudly, as though he might at any moment die. Everyone around him gives him space, but they are still unsure what for.

.   .   .

Then suddenly he appears to be bleeding out of his ears so that they want to go forward and help him. But they step back, as a tiny spider-like organism exits through one ear, with three domes on its back, or on its head, they are not sure. Nobody is quick enough to tramp the creature, just watching in amazement as it scurries back up the stairs, probably needing the comfort of the cold that it left behind.

They decide to leave it. It will not survive the heat of the explosion anyway. Instead, they help a disoriented Grant Chambers to his feet again, sure now that they have Chambers, the man, with them. He cannot speak, but they just reassure him that everything will be okay now, and they make their way down the rest of the stairs.

The army moves quickly to disconnect the computer hardware that they need. They stuff it in their pockets, and in every flap on the clothing that they have on. There is no time to waste, nobody even speaking to one another. They have to get out of the building.

By the time they make it to the outside of the building, they create as much distance between it and themselves, but not so much so that they cannot watch the front of the building. They wait anxiously for Alexis and Tucker to come out, but they don't. A debate rages on, on the outside of the World Government's headquarters, and they wonder if they should not perhaps go in and try to find them. But Tucker was clear on his instruction. Everybody must get out of the building.

Security guards watch from the outside too, none of them willing to risk their lives for a government that wasn't really theirs anyway. The whole world watches anxiously for the three, Tucker, Alexis, and C-lo to exit. But still, nothing.

The sun has come out now and hangs high in the sky. Hundreds of thousands of New Yorkers have descended on the building too, armed, and ready to fight for their lives, and for the lives of their families. But right now it's just a waiting game. So they wait, and wait, and wait.

The building starts to shake so that everybody moves back a little more. They wait, still anticipating the exit, still nothing. They doubt that their heroes have made it, and that they will ever see them again. But still, nobody can bring themselves to leave the general area around the building.

They continue to watch as the building seems to rumble, and then settle before rumbling again. Chloe cannot look, she cannot watch. She has prepared herself for the day that she will lose her brother in the line of duty, but nothing could have prepared her for the way she is feeling, to watch it happening right in front of her.

She turns to the muscle that is still holding her close and buries her head in his broad chest. She wishes that she had told her brother how much she loves him. She wishes that she was open with him from the start about how she felt about her parents dying, and about his chosen profession. She wishes a lot of things, but none of them matter now. The building seems to heave a heavy sigh of relief, before it comes crashing down in a systematic order, from the penthouse.

. . .

Still, they watch, waiting, anticipation thick in the air, but everyone knowing that nobody, human or otherwise, could survive the collapse of en entire building. They suddenly wish that it was like in the movies, where the hero emerges from the rubble unscathed. But nothing, and no one comes out of the building. People start to remove their hats, bowing the heads low.

But just then C-lo appears laptop in hand, a broad grin on his face. He is followed by Alexis and Tucker, who are locked in an embrace but still running. They need to get as far away from the building as possible, not sure just how complete the destruction is yet to be. They made it out, but how?

Nobody seems to care how a loud cheering ensuing that fills the streets of New York. Yes, they've probably set the clock back by a thousand years, but so what. They're alive, and they will be alive to try and do things better this time around.

Tucker looks at his sister, who is still unable to look at him. He cracks a smile that lets her know that he forgives her. She can't restrain herself any longer, running to him and embracing him and Alexis at the same time. Perhaps it's not such a bad thing, to go back in time, after all!

ABOUT THE AUTHOR

Candra Aubrey is an emerging erotica author of many erotica kinks and sub-genres. Be sure to check out other books and leave a review if this story got you hot!

Visit my blog at Candra Aubrey's Blog

Join my newsletter for the exclusive Candra Aubrey's Newsletter

Sign up for Free Stories from Xplicit Press Authors

Xplicit Press Author Updates

Like Xplicit Press on Facebook

Follow Xplicit Press on Twitter

Readers: I want to expand a few of the stories to see where the characters can be explored further. If there are any of the stories that you would like to read more about again, I'd love to hear from you!

Keep In Touch
Candra Aubrey
info@candraaubrey.com